NELSON TELSON
The Story of a True Blue Blood

Story & Pictures by Heidi Mayo

Nelson Telson – The Story of a True Blue Blood is a work of fiction. Although some of the places are real, the names, characters, interiors, and incidents are solely a product of the author's imagination or are used fictitiously. Any resemblance to actual events, interiors, or persons, living or dead, is purely coincidental.

For Jane & Thomas
and all of the creatures on this watery world

Contents

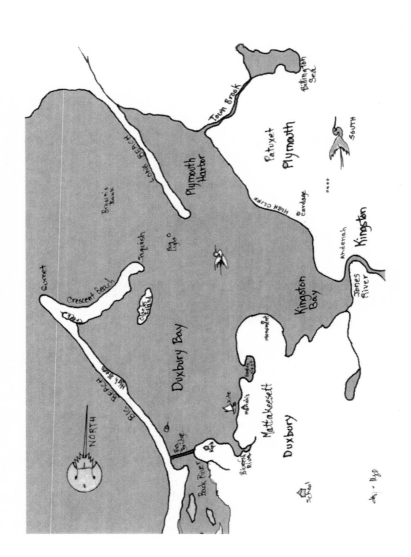

Chapter I
Nelson

It was the end of August, and the sky was clear back-to-school blue. Mariah's mother had parked on the bay side of the beach in the lee of the dunes to keep out of the steady sea breeze. The sand was warm and golden, but a snap in the air signaled summer's passing, sending a shiver of goose bumps across Mariah Miller's tanned arms.

She was going into the sixth grade this year, into a new school, in a new town, in a new state, knowing no one. The first day loomed closer as the air got drier and the sun sank lower. She kept imagining that first day of school, being forced to stand up and introduce herself to the class. She had done it so many times before, in other classrooms, in other towns, in other states, each September of her life. Her cheeks got red just thinking about it.

Glistening sunlight sharpened the tips of beach grass as they danced in the breeze that swept Mariah's hair across her face. When she stepped over a mound of dried seaweed something crunched under her foot. It was the dried shell of a baby horseshoe crab, all golden and crinkly. She hadn't noticed them before, hundreds of small crab shells strewn about in the seaweed like meatballs in a big pile of black pasta.

She was collecting the golden shells along the edge of the marsh grass when she spied something interesting. It was flat and shiny, and had edges that came to a point. An arrowhead! She turned it over and over in her hand feeling how it had been smoothed by time. She ran to her mother's beach chair. "Mom," she said, opening her hand. "Look what I found!"

Mariah's mother sat back in the chair with the big fat novel she had been reading for the past few days. Since she hadn't lifted her head away from the page, Mariah thrust her hand between her mom's sunglasses and the book. "Hmm," said her mother.

"Mom," said Mariah, "it's an arrowhead! You know, from the Indians who lived here a long time ago!"

"Actually, it's a spearhead," said her mom, peering over her glasses and squinting at it. "Arrowheads are smaller. And we don't call them Indians anymore. Indians are from India; your spearhead belonged to a Native American." Her mother took the stone from Mariah's hand, inspected it for a moment, and handed it back. "Very nice," she said, returning to the book.

Mariah held the spearhead tightly in her fist as she explored the marsh. Out of the corner of her eye she thought she saw something moving down by the water. When she looked up she saw nothing out of the ordinary, just some dark rocks scattered in the muddy sand. The tide was low, so it wasn't the small rippling waves farther out or the white glint of a seagull coasting in the distant sky.

Thinking how pretty they'd look all lined up on the mantle in her new bedroom, she gathered the shells until her hands and arms were so full she dropped one or two every time she bent down to pick up another. Combing the tide line for a littered plastic bag or some other container to put them in, she found the perfect thing half buried in the blackened heaps of seaweed. It was the hollow shell of a big, old horseshoe crab, strong and rigid, dark as ebony.

Wherever she looked, she saw more and more shells. But something kept drawing her attention back to the water. She left her crab bowl up on the beach and headed down to investigate.

Splashing through a tidal pool she stubbed her toe on a rock, and the spearhead flew from her hand and landed on the wet sand. She limped over to find it pointing, like an arrow on a map. It directed her eyes across the sand to an upside-down horseshoe crab that looked like a jagged rock with ten wildly wiggling legs. It was rotating its tail, which was not long and pointed like other horseshoe crabs' but broken off at the end. It was attempting to flip over, and drawing a design in the damp sand that looked like a quarter moon.

As Mariah reached down to pick up her spearhead she heard a small deep sound coming from the animal. At first it sounded like bubbles popping. But then, she thought she heard it say, "Help! Help!"

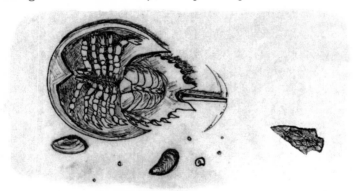

Gently, she flipped it over. If she didn't know better, she could have sworn she heard it say, "Thank you."

Looking around to make sure no one was paying attention, she leaned down closer, inspecting the broken tail. "Looks like you broke your sword," she whispered. She always talked to animals that way, but never expected them to talk back.

"Not a sword," the voice creaked, "it's a telson."

Mariah smacked her forehead with an open palm. Oh my gosh, she thought. I'm crazy!

"Mariah!" her mother called.

She was so startled by her mother's voice, the

spearhead popped out of her hand again. "Put your hat on, dear," she said.

Mariah leaned down, and whispered to the crab, "a *what*-son?"

All she could hear was a bubbly sound. She must have imagined that it had talked. Silly, she thought, of course horseshoe crabs can't talk.

Her mom glanced up from the book and called down to the water again, "Your hat, please." Ever since her mom had a cancerous sore blamed on the sun removed from her nose, she was always lecturing Mariah that it's never too early to start caring for your skin.

"Okay," Mariah said. Disappointed, she reached down and picked up her spearhead.

"A telson," said the creature.

Mariah's eyes widened as she looked at the spearhead in her hand. She placed it carefully on the sand. "Could you repeat that, please?"

All she heard was the lapping of small waves. She picked up the spearhead again.

"It is a telson," said the creaky voice, "That is what my tail is called."

"Oh my goodness," she said, shocked that she was actually talking to this animal, worried that she was crazy, but liking it so much that she wanted to keep the conversation going. She clenched the spearhead in her fist. "How did you break it?"

"Break what?"

"Your tail, your telson, I mean."

"I didn't break it; I sacrificed it in an act of altruism to a beakless great blue heron who is now forever grateful."

Mariah was flabbergasted. The crab went on about the importance of giving to those in need while Mariah shut her eyes as hard as she could, and then opened them slowly to make sure she wasn't dreaming.

She stood there shaking her head in disbelief: A talking horseshoe crab, and a philanthropic one at that! Her mom had just said that word the other day, philanthropic. She said it meant showing concern for others and giving to charity. Giving half of your tail to a beakless heron certainly was philanthropic. She tried to imagine the heron, such a majestic bird, its long neck poised elegantly above the water, with a horseshoe crab's tail for a beak.

Well, if she was going to be talking to a horseshoe crab, she might as well ask. "How did you attach it to the heron's mouth?"

"I didn't," it said. "Some mussels pitched in, and the sandpipers helped. They are very helpful birds, you know."

Mariah listened in disbelief. It was too incredible! The horseshoe crab went on chatting as if it talked to kids on the beach every day.

"Sandpipers?" She had seen the small brown birds scampering about the shore, and now it was telling her that they were helpful? What next? She looked at the spearhead in her hand. "Wait a sec," she said as she knelt down and put it on the sand. "Sandpipers?" she said again.

All she could hear was a bubbly sound. She snapped the spearhead up in her hand. "...very helpful animals," she heard it say. "They glued my half telson to the heron's beak stub with the adhesive mussels use to stick themselves to rocks and each other. It is one of nature's strongest glues, you know. Then they tied it with string to hold it until the glue set. They found the string on a stale balloon that landed on the beach."

"Wow," was all Mariah could say.

"Now when he dines, Aaron, that's his name, stabs a fish with his prosthesis, flips it into the air, and sends it right down his gullet!" The horseshoe crab seemed happy to have someone to talk to, someone who listened attentively. It told Mariah that most creatures don't listen very well at all.

"Mariah, your hat, dear," her mom called from the beach chair.

"In a minute," Mariah said impatiently. She didn't want to move. She was afraid to take her eyes off that animal for fear it would crawl back into the bay and disappear forever.

"Now!" the voice behind the book said. Sometimes Mariah thought her mom must have x-ray vision, always seeing everything but never seeming to look away from her book.

She told the crab to please stay put; she'd be right

back. There were so many things she wanted to ask him. As she trudged through the soft sand up to the canvas bag, she began to get a greedy, impatient feeling. It was like rushing to get in line for something, and not knowing if there might be any left when her turn finally came. She wanted to find out everything that crab knew.

The stiff breeze raced from the ocean over the top of the dunes, and the waves crashed hard on the other side. It was chilly standing up there in the wind, and the length of her shadow reminded her again that school was starting in a few days. Quickly, she pulled her sweatshirt on and headed back down to the water.

"The hat," her mother said.

Mariah pivoted on her heel and sent a plume of sand flying off behind her as she marched back to the bag for her blue baseball cap. It was a Red Sox cap her dad had given her when they moved. He said that now that they lived near Boston again they could be real Red Sox fans. Mariah didn't care either way, but she liked the cap because her dad had given it to her.

She plucked a little crab shell up by the telson and twirled it between her fingers as she ran back to her big, live, *talking* crab as fast she could.

What a relief! It hadn't moved an inch. She looked from the little dead one in her hand to the sturdy, dark brown creature. It had a few barnacles growing on its shell and a small piece of green seaweed attached to the base of its broken tail.

Holding the spearhead was like holding a wish, a wish that the magic was still working. "Looks like you've got a few guests here," she touched its shell lightly. "You've got two barnacles and a nice piece of seaweed growing on your shell." She crossed her fingers on one hand and clenched the spearhead in the other, hoping it would talk again.

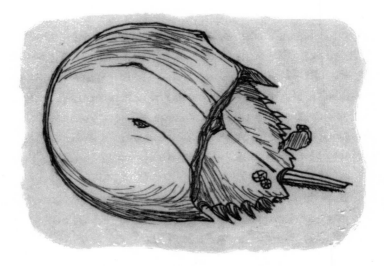

"Do I?" it replied to her delight. "Well, I'm happy to have them along for the ride. Anything that wants to attach itself to my carapace is certainly welcome."

"Carapace," she repeated. "That's your shell?"

"Indeed," said the horseshoe crab.

She didn't want to seem nosy, but she was very curious. It seemed so wise. "If you don't mind my asking...are you are boy or girl?"

"I am neither. I am an adult male *Limulus*

polyphemus, probably one of the most misunderstood creatures on this earth."

"Misunderstood?"

"Just look at me! Humans somehow think we, with our sharp telsons and full suit of armor, are evil or dangerous. The truth is, we *Limulus* are among the most pleasant creatures on earth!"

"I agree," said Mariah. "You sure are a pleasant crab."

"And, then you go and call me a crab! I am an arthropod; I'll admit to that, but not a crab at all."

Mariah was dumbfounded. The horseshoe crab went on and on. "I'm more like a tick or spider, only a distant relation to the true crustaceans, those crabs and lobsters and shrimps." He heaved a bubbly sigh. "But we're all brothers and sisters in this watery world. You too, young human."

Mariah knew what he meant. She could feel the whole round world under her feet, and the liquid home of her new friend flowing full circle.

The crab made a noise, *abble bidle,* interrupting her dreamy thoughts. "What? I'm sorry, I didn't catch that."

"Have you a title?" he repeated.

"Title?" She wasn't sure what he meant. That animal seemed to use some pretty fancy words. "Oh, you mean a name," she said using her best manners. "My name is Mariah Miller, and I am very glad to meet you, sir."

"You can call me Nelson, Nelson Telson."

"You are named after your tail?"

"It follows," he said wryly.

Mariah giggled, and then giggled some more when she realized she was actually joking with this dark brown, tank-like creature who impressed her with his fine sensibility and rich vocabulary. She glanced around the beach. All the late season sunbathers and picnickers were at a safe distance. Her mother was deeply involved in her book.

She lowered her voice. "How do you defend yourself, now that your telson is broken?"

Nelson answered thoughtfully. "We have no natural enemies. A telson serves no purpose as a weapon of defense or offense, which is why I could share part of mine with Aaron. My only armament is this tough old shell, but even this cannot save me from an inconsiderate human, such as that little one on this beach who accosted me."

Mariah looked down the shore to see a kid waving a red plastic shovel and chasing a small flock of seagulls. "Oh, is that how you got upside down?"

"Indeed," he scowled, "and if I had been just a little less generous and kept a half-inch more of my telson, I would have turned aright and been gone from this beach some time ago. And we never would have met!"

That was unthinkable. She really liked Nelson. He was easy to talk to, and she didn't feel the least bit shy with him. She felt she had finally made a friend in this new town.

"Mariah," her mom called, "it's time we got going."

She looked up to see that her mother had not closed the book yet, which meant that she must be near the end of a chapter. Mariah knew she had at least another minute or two before she really had to start moving.

"I wish I could stay and talk to you more. There's so much I want to ask you. Will I ever see you again?"

Nelson gave a small laugh. "You really don't know much about horseshoe crabs, do you?"

"No, I don't."

"We *limulus* never travel more than a few miles from our spawning place, the place where we were born. Sometimes the tides and rough waters take us for a ride, but generally, we stick around."

Mariah was flustered thinking of her friend Nelson going off a couple of miles into the bay. Why, he could end up in Kingston, or Plymouth! She'd never find him. "But, but how will I ever get to see you again?"

"We'll just make a plan," he said. "I'll meet you right here at low water."

"How about tomorrow?" She was anxious. She could ride her bike, and her mom would be happy she wasn't moping around the house. Then she remembered that she was going sailing with her dad and had a dentist appointment in the afternoon. She looked up to see her mother put the book in her beach bag. "No, that's no good. How about Friday?"

" Friday? What's that?"

"The day after tomorrow."

"Two suns," Nelson said.

Mariah understood. "Yes, the second sun. Low tide, Friday," she said excitedly, holding her spearhead tightly. "It's a date!"

"A date?" Nelson was confused. "Hum," she heard him mumble as she skipped off, "maybe she thinks I like fruit."

Mariah shook out her beach towel sending a shiny mist of sand into the breeze. She scooped up her horseshoe crab bowl, and headed for the Jeep.

As they bounced along the sandy road towards the bridge Mariah's mom glanced over at the bowl of shells. "So," she said, "what was so interesting down there at the water today?"

"Oh, nothing," said Mariah. She held the spearhead in her hand and her secret close to her heart. Nobody would believe her anyway; they'd just think she was making up one of her outlandish stories.

That night Mariah opened the journal her mother had given her when they had moved. She was almost afraid to write. What if somebody read it? They'd think she was nuts. But when her mom had given it to her, she had said that a personal journal was a sacred thing, and nobody will read it unless invited. She opened the cover and uncapped the nice pen that came with it.

She wrote *Private Property Keep Out* in big

bold letters on the first page, flipped to the next and began her journal.

Today was the weirdest day of my life. I found a magic spearhead from the Indians and then a horseshoe crab talked to me! I'm not kidding. When I was holding the spearhead I could hear the crab talk, but when I dropped it I couldn't hear him. He is a very nice animal and he told me a lot about being a horseshoe crab. He gave part of his tail called a <u>telson</u> to a great blue heron. No kidding. That's why he couldn't flip over which is really lucky because if he had a longer tail I never would have met him. I'm going to the beach on Friday at low tide. I hope I can find him and he'll talk. Maybe I'm crazy but this really happened.

Chapter II
The Kite

Mariah stepped quickly to keep up with her dad as they headed down to the end of the lane. His life jacket swung from the oars on his shoulder, back and forth with each step of his long legs. The Swiss Army knife she had found in her Christmas stocking last year dangled from the clip on her belt loop. She patted her pocket where she had put a safety pin to make sure the spearhead wouldn't fall out.

The *Kite* rocked gently at the mooring, early sun glinting off her shiny parts, and little waves of clean white reflections radiating from her hull. Mr. Miller flipped the dinghy over and dragged it through the eelgrass to the water. He groaned and rubbed his back. "You okay, Dad?" she asked.

"Just a little backache, honey," he said, holding the dinghy's stern while Mariah got in with the oars. When she was on the seat, he pushed hard and jumped in all at once, lifting Mariah up as though she were on the high end of a seesaw. She rowed carefully, turning now and then, and when she got close enough, she pushed one oar forward and pulled the other back to swing the dinghy alongside. "A perfect landing," said her dad.

Mr. Miller hoisted the sail while Mariah climbed onto the foredeck and tied the dinghy to the mooring. The *Kite* was a pretty little catboat, a Beetle Cat, that they called a Bug. Mariah's dad and her Uncle Joe had raced her in the bay when they were boys. Whenever the Millers had moved, the *Kite* had come along with them on a trailer. When they were on the road back to Massachusetts, Mariah's dad said the *Kite* was happy to be going home, and so was he.

The sail flapped impatiently, pushing the boat back and forth like a compass needle pointing to the wind. Her dad watched as Mariah prepared to cast off. She studied the wind just as he had taught her. She looked at how the other boats were swinging on their moorings, checked the yarn telltale tied to the stay, and then, with a very serious look on her face, she stuck her index finger in her mouth to wet it and then held it up in the air, feeling the breeze. Her dad chuckled.

"Out of the east," she said, "onshore."

Mr. Miller nodded in agreement. Once he had taught her something, he sat back and let her take charge. That spring as they put a new coat of salmon pink paint on the boat's deck, he ceremoniously handed over command of the *Kite* to "the next generation," which meant Mariah was now the skipper and she steered the boat.

"Let's go around Clark's Island," she said.

"Good idea," said Mr. Miller as he dropped the centerboard.

Mariah cast off the mooring, hopped down into the cockpit, and pushed the tiller hard. "Dad, you take the main."

"Aye Aye," he said, reaching for the thick line and pulling it in while Mariah pushed the tiller back and forth a few times, filling the sail with air and sending them off toward Eagles Nest. Her dad trimmed the sail as Mariah headed the *Kite* higher into the wind.

They sailed along until Mariah called out, "Ready about, hard to lee!" and pushed the tiller to starboard – the right side of the boat. Her dad ducked as the boom swung over the top of his head, and the *Kite* headed for the Big Bridge. She looked over at her dad who was scrunched in the cockpit, his long legs bent at the knees like he was trying to fit in a bathtub. The steady wind pushed the sandy hair from his forehead and made him squint.

The wind began to build and turn as they sailed across the bay, right for the spot where she had met Nelson the day before. She imagined him out there under the water doing horseshoe crab things, crawling along the muddy bottom, eating worms. And then she thought about how nice it would be to not have to go to school on Monday. "Animals have all the luck," she said.

"What's that, honey?" her dad called over the wind.

She raised her voice. "I was just thinking about how nice it would be to just be an animal and not have to be a person. I said, 'Animals have all the luck.'"

Her dad squinted at her. "What do you mean? Some animals have a pretty hard life."

"No," she disagreed, "they just *are*. They don't have to do all the silly things people do. They just *are*." A gull was riding the breeze above them. "Look at him," she said pointing. "He's just being a gull."

Mr. Miller laughed.

"They don't have to go to school. They don't have to wear clothes. They don't have to move all the time..."

"Mariah," said her dad, "I told you this was our last move. And I'm sorry we had to move so often, but that was part of my job. I promise you, this time we are staying put."

She hadn't meant to make him feel bad. "I know," she said, only half believing it.

"And besides," he said, "animals move around all the time. Birds fly south in the winter and north in the spring; salmon go upstream to spawn; deer move all over the place to forage for food, even monarch butterflies migrate."

With a nod, she conceded; he was right.

They had almost reached the beach. The wind was blowing harder now, and the waves were big and sloppy. "Ready, about," she commanded, and they ducked into the cockpit as the boat crossed through the wind, and the boom came over. Mariah's dad slacked the main while she headed the *Kite* on a broad reach along the beach.

Her dad pointed out the landmarks, telling her about the snowy owls in the winter at High Pines, and the lazy summer afternoons swimming in Gurnet Creek. He had grown up there, so whenever they went sailing or drove around in the car, Mr. Miller acted as tour guide, naming the streets and places, and telling her stories of his childhood.

The boat lurched ahead in the stiff breeze towards the tip of the island. "Used to be a big heron rookery on this end of the island. Gulls nested there, too. Now they're all gone. Foxes," he said.

Mariah held onto the tiller with both hands, struggling against the forces of wind and waves. She was too busy trying to steer to chat about gulls and foxes. Just then the boat fell down a trough, burying the bow and sending water washing over the deck. Her dad offered to take over, but Mariah refused. Now that she was the skipper, she was going to steer no matter how hard it got. The boom lifted and fell, shooting the *Kite* forward with each wave. Her father showed her where to make landfall so they could reef the sail to make it smaller so the boat would be easier to handle.

"Jibe ho!" she hollered as she ducked down and pushed the tiller, feeling the wind cross behind her, readying herself for whatever might happen when the sail slammed over with all of its power. Her dad didn't seem worried at all as he skillfully trimmed the main and then let it out slowly, taming the wind, and making her feel safe.

Now she had to figure out how to land the *Kite* without crashing into the island. She wanted to show her dad that she was capable. She wanted to ask him what to do, but even more, she wanted to show him she could do it. She had to make up her mind quickly as the boat was flying straight for the island.

She steered as far downwind as she could without jibing, past the sandy landing place, and when it seemed the right moment, she yelled, "Rounding up!" and pushed the tiller hard to bring the *Kite* up into the wind, to land sideways on the shore. Her dad let go of the main, and the boat glided onto the beach. Mariah let out a big sigh of relief.

"Good job," Mr. Miller said, jumping out and pulling the *Kite* ashore.

Everything seemed so still now that they were on

land. Mariah used her jackknife to cut a clean end on the reefing line so it could fit through the grommet on the sail. They were working together, rolling the bottom part of the sail and tying it down, when a man came strolling towards them from an old white clapboard house. "Is that you, Mike Miller?" He reached out and shook hands. "Long time," he said.

Mariah's dad introduced her to the man, Jeff, an old friend of Uncle Joe's, and then they went on talking about old times when they were kids. Mariah stood by, half listening.

"Hey," said Jeff, "Remember that time Joe and Tim and I got all those horseshoe crabs?" Mariah's ears perked up.

She didn't want to ask, but she had Nelson on her mind and she couldn't help herself. "Got all those horseshoe crabs?"

"Yep," he said. "There was a bounty on them, and we got a nickel apiece for every crab we collected."

"A bounty?"

"Yep, they were everywhere. They were considered a nuisance. But people have learned better. They're real valuable now."

Mariah couldn't imagine it. How could a horseshoe crab be a nuisance? "What did you do with them?"

"We brought them down to the harbor master in wheelbarrows. We must have done about six loads one day."

"What happened to them?"

"I'm not sure," said Jeff scratching his head. "But it was a lot of money for us kids to make back then. We bought a lot of ice cream that summer!"

Mariah felt sad all of a sudden. In fact, the whole business made her uneasy as she imagined wheelbarrows full of Nelson's relatives being carted down to the waterfront. She didn't want to hear anymore about it so she moved off, looking around at the old houses, windblown lawns, and paths leading to places she had never been.

"Can I go exploring, Dad?"

"Sure," he said, "go up that path until you find the graveyard I told you about. Pulpit Rock is just on the other side. But don't be gone long. We need to get underway soon."

Mariah ran off up between the cool cedars. The stout trees sheltered her from the wind, and she felt as though she had entered a new world. A gray fox trotted into the path ahead of her. "Hello," Mariah whispered excitedly under her breath.

The fox turned, saw her, and darted off into the underbrush. She ran after it hoping to get a better look, but it had disappeared.

She slowed her pace as she reached the cemetery. It was dark and shady, surrounded by tall trees. The clayish dirt was hard packed from the footsteps of many years. Unclasping the safety pin, she brought the spearhead out of her pocket. I'll bet the Indians liked it here, she said to herself, "the natives," she whispered, remembering what her mother had said.

"They did..." said the fox in a soft, matronly voice as she stepped cautiously out from behind an old gravestone. She eyed Mariah and added knowingly, "for the most part."

Her fur was tawny, like the dried tufts of grass bordering the graveyard. The fox met her surprise with a bold gaze.

Mariah gasped. Yesterday, a horseshoe crab, and today, a fox! She was speechless.

The fox didn't seem to care. "This is a sacred place." She put a delicate paw forward and tipped her muzzle to the ground as if to genuflect. "All places are sacred."

Mariah thought about that. Yes, all places are sacred.

"The English settlers used this island not only as a

place of worship, but later this sacred place was a prison for the People of The First Light, a prison for those who tried to feed their hungry by sharing bounty held by white men over harsh winters. People of The First Light know not of ownership, only of sharing."

"People of The First Light," Mariah repeated. "Who are the people of the first light? Can I meet them?"

"Most died from diseases that the settlers brought with them in their ships; some were sold into slavery; few remain today. They shared this land and all of its gifts."

Mariah looked at the spearhead in her hand, and a wave of understanding washed over her. For the first time, she thought of land the way an animal does, and the idea of a person owning it made no sense at all. It surely wouldn't make sense to a migratory bird, a fish or horseshoe crab, or any other creatures or people that move around to find food. If a storm can wash away land, then how could anyone own it? "All of the earth belongs to all of the creatures," Mariah blurted out.

The fox nodded agreement, and trotted off. Mariah followed her through a shaded path to a huge gray rock in the center of a sloping field. Cedars and oaks stood around the field like sentinels. Four little foxes stumbled into the clearing, nipping and chasing each other.

"Oh," squealed Mariah, "they're so cute!" She knelt on the ground and held her hand out as if to befriend a dog, but the kits just ignored her. "May I touch them?

"Please, no," said the fox politely. "You are a fine and honorable creature yourself, but your species in general cannot be trusted."

"I know," she said, embarrassed to be a human, associated with Uncle Joe and Jeff and the dreadful things they had done to all of those horseshoe crabs just to get ice cream money. She patted the big rock with her opened palm. It was at least three times her height and almost as big as a house. The stone had warmed under the morning sun. Mariah climbed up on it and peered down at the fox. "How is it that you can talk to me?"

"It is you who speaks to me."

The sound of her dad's shrill, two-fingered whistle came over the woods and echoed in the clearing. The little foxes stopped playing and stood at wide-eyed attention, waiting for direction from their mother. Mariah stood up high on the rock and yelled through cupped hands, "Coming, Dad!"

When she turned back to say goodbye, the fox and her kits had disappeared.

Chapter III
Weather

M r. Miller was relaxing in his easy chair. The evening news was on television, but he couldn't see it because he was reading the newspaper. Mariah went to the bookshelf and got the H book of the encyclopedia. When she walked by his chair, he tossed his newspaper onto the hassock, patted his knee, and invited her to hop on.

"That was quite a sail this morning, eh?"

Mariah nodded. "Wasn't so bad after we reefed the sail."

She was small for eleven, almost twelve, and happily still small enough to sit on her dad's lap. He squeezed her tightly and said, just as he had ever since she could remember, "Maaariiiaahhhh...," stretching her name out so it sounded like a cat's meow. He sang the same old song he always did, a song she'd heard from an old cartoon. *Mariah, Mariah, I'm waiting for you...* And then he made up a silly rhyme. This time he sang, "...to tell me a tall tale about the first day of school!"

"Oh, Daddy, you know it doesn't start until Monday," she tried not to whine. "Did you have to remind me?" Just the thought of it, the thought of being stuck inside at a desk in a room with a bunch of strangers, gave her a bad feeling all over.

He asked her what she was looking up, and why she wasn't using the computer. "What, no Google?"

"Mom's on it," she answered, "and I like these old books."

He watched as she flipped the pages until she found the listing for Horseshoe Crab.

"Oh," he said, "those ugly things with the pointy tails that stick up in the mud? You wouldn't want to step on one!"

"No, I wouldn't. I might hurt the poor thing," she said, all persnickety. She leaned against him, looking at the picture of a horseshoe crab just like Nelson only it didn't have barnacles and seaweed on it, and its tail wasn't broken. The caption read: horseshoe crab (*Limulus polyphemus*). She whispered to herself, *lim-u-lus poly-fee-mus*, just like she'd heard Nelson say it. "They eat small mollusks and worms." She wanted to tell her dad about Nelson and the fox but thought better of it. Maybe it had been all in her imagination.

Her dad pointed at the picture. "That tail looks dangerous to me."

"Well, it says here that they only use the telson, that's the tail, to move around in the mud, dig nests, and hitch a ride with a partner to mate in the spring and summer." Mariah perused the article thoughtfully. "But they left something out."

She checked her dad's eyes to make sure he was

paying attention. Sure enough, he was looking at the TV weatherman pointing at a map of the region and talking about an approaching tropical depression and gale warnings. Nelson was right, most creatures aren't very good listeners.

She tapped the book to get his attention. "They use their telson to flip over when they've been turned upside down. I saw one do it yesterday on the beach. Well, he tried to do it but his telson was broken off, so I helped him."

Mr. Miller pointed to an old scrapbook on the shelf. "Grab that for me, please." Mariah got the album and hopped back on her dad's lap. He winced. His back hurt.

"Remember Jeff, on the island?" Her dad opened the scrapbook and leafed through the crumbling black pages of photos and clippings stuck on with deteriorating Scotch tape until he found what he was looking for. He pointed to the picture. "There used to be a lot of horseshoe crabs around here when I was a kid. Too many. That's why Jeff and your Uncle Joe collected the bounty. A nickel apiece, big money back then."

Mariah stared at the yellowed newspaper clipping. The smiling summer faces of her Uncle Joe and his barefoot pals looked out at her, with their tanned shoulders and sun-bleached hair. They were standing with their wheelbarrows in front of a mountain of horseshoe crabs. "They were a nuisance," her dad said.

"Oh, Daddy," she cried. "They are not!"

"What did they do with them?" she asked, hoping against hope that they took them somewhere else and let them go.

" I think," her dad replied, "they were buried in a big pit."

She had read in the encyclopedia that in some coastal communities horseshoe crabs had been ground up for fertilizer. The thought of the slaughter of all those innocent, helpless horseshoe crabs made Mariah so angry and sick she could hardly speak. She fought back tears as she imagined somebody carelessly tossing her friend Nelson onto a pile of writhing horseshoe crabs bound for a fertilizer plant! How could she ever like her Uncle Joe again?

"Did a horseshoe crab ever hurt you?" She didn't wait for his reply. "No! No wonder there are so few of them now," she said in a huff. "People are *so stupid*!" She knocked the scrapbook to the floor as she jumped off her dad's lap, ran up the stairs to her room which she hadn't gotten used to yet, and slammed the door.

Her new room had old wallpaper with pink rosebuds on it. It must have been the daughter's room, of the family that lived there before. There was something about the pink color that bothered Mariah.

Just then, in her mood, she had decided that she hated that fake pink color of those stupid wallpaper roses. She had to admit though; there was one very good thing about her new room. It had a fireplace in it. It was a real working fireplace from the olden days, with an iron arm that swung from two eyelets sunk into the mortar. Her dad had promised to teach her how to use it when the weather got cold, and her mom said she'd buy her a kettle so she could make tea in her room.

Mariah picked up her journal and wrote furiously.

Today we went sailing and it got very windy. We stopped on Clark's Island to reef the sail. Dad met up with an old friend, a horseshoe crab killer. He and Uncle Joe got tons of them and they were killed. I hate Uncle Joe. I can't believe that people can be so mean and stupid. I went to the graveyard and Pulpit Rock where the English pilgrims had church. You're not going to believe this, but a fox talked to me! Really. She talked about the people of the first light and how they shared and how all places are sacred and all places belong to all creatures. When I hold the spearhead I can hear animals talk to me. This is the second time. Tomorrow

I'm going to the beach. I hope Nelson will talk to me again. I hope I'm not just imagining this.

There was dampness in the air, and as Mariah dozed off she smelled the smoke of all of the fires that had burned in her fireplace over the past two centuries.

She dreamed she was in a symphony orchestra, playing a triangle in the percussion section. Next to her, the booming kettledrum demanded the attention. The piece was one she had heard in music class at school, a piece the teacher used as an example of music's imagery. Deep in her sleeping mind she knew it was Friday, and she had to finish up there at the symphony and ride her bike to the beach to meet Nelson. She was dreaming of her bike wheels rumbling over the wooden planks of the big bridge as she heard the louder rumbling of a car approaching from behind. Suddenly an earsplitting crash woke her.

She sat bolt upright in her bed as a flash of white light fell across the wallpaper roses. Waves of rain pelted her windows. She smelled the smell of the old fires and heard the wind whistle in bursts down her chimney. Lightning cracked so loudly it shook the house. Thunder rumbled and boomed. The "tropical depression" that the TV weatherman had been talking about had arrived as a big and powerful storm. Any other day she would have welcomed the wild weather, but not today. She had plans, and she wasn't going to let a little bad weather get in the way. Her alarm clock read 7:30; she planned to wait until ten o'clock and leave just before low tide. Hopefully the storm would be gone by then.

Mariah crept past her mother towards the mudroom. She had never lived in a house with a mudroom before. When they had just moved into the house and her mother had told her to leave her jacket in the mudroom, she had laughed because the name sounded so funny. "I mean it, young lady," her mother had said sternly, thinking Mariah was being a smart aleck.

"Why is it called a mudroom?" Mariah giggled at the thought of having a room just for mud.

"Because, that's where you leave your muddy boots and wet clothes. Farmhouses had them and this was a farmhouse. So, kindly hang up your jacket in the mudroom." That was just two months ago, and now the mudroom was filled with the family's jackets and sweatshirts and hats and beach towels and tennis racquets and golf clubs and shopping bags and sandals and boots and rain gear.

She heard her mother turn the page of the new book she had started yesterday, a big fat one with fancy curlicue lettering on the cover. Mariah felt the front pocket of her dungarees to make sure she had the spearhead. She wanted to show it to Nelson. As quietly as possible, she lifted her yellow slicker off the hook and slipped into a pair of too-large rubber boots.

So far, so good, she thought as she opened the back door slowly and tiptoed out. Just then a powerful gust of wet wind grabbed the screen door from her and slammed it against the side of the house.

"Mariah dear," her mother called from behind her book. "Where are you going?"

"Just out for a little while," she called as she closed the door.

"It might be too stormy," her mom called.

"The storm is clearing," said Mariah. Lucky for her that her mother was so involved with the book she wasn't paying attention or she might have told Mariah that she couldn't go.

The thunder and lightning had stopped and the rain seemed to have diminished. Mariah hoped for a clearing sky as she pedaled the mile to the bridge. The houses along the road were wet and shiny and dotted with shards of green leaves that the wind had torn from the late summer trees.

It began to rain again as she coasted toward the head of the bridge. Now that she was out of the shelter of the trees and houses along the street, it was difficult to pedal against the strong wind that blasted across Back River and over the bay.

The rain started coming down so heavily she

couldn't even see the other end of the long bridge. Her face was drenched, her feet were getting wet, and chilly water had begun to trickle down the back of her neck.

Pedaling with all of her might, Mariah had gotten halfway across the bridge when a huge gust of wind knocked her off her bicycle. She tumbled and skidded along the planks. Her boot flew off, and her bare ankle was scraped raw on the edge of the wooden sidewalk before she finally slid to a halt. Rumpled and stinging, she gathered herself up from the slippery planks and limped back to the rail to retrieve her bike.

Getting back on, she noticed that her front tire was nearly flat. It must have been damaged when it struck the sidewalk planks. Now how was she going to get across the bridge?

She looked across the angry water to where Nelson should be waiting for her. The strong wind swept spume over whitecaps. Her ankle really hurt as she pulled the boot back on. Both feet were numb and soggy.

Crushed, she sat down on the wet sidewalk, getting her pants all the wetter. She put her face in her hands and started to cry. Tears warmed her cool cheeks for a moment before they got mixed up with the storm on her face. She reached into her pocket to make sure she hadn't lost the spearhead; the warm stone felt like comfort in her cold hand. Hard rain pelted the back of her yellow slicker, tap, tap, tapping on her shoulders and telling her to turn around and go home.

Clenching the spearhead so as not to lose it through the cracks, she got up to assess the damage. A tiny peeping sound rose beneath the howling of the wind. There on the lower rung of the wooden railing, blinking rain from its eyes, was a disheveled little sandpiper.

"Oh my goodness!" she whispered. "You must be lost. Are you all right?" Mariah was concerned for the little brownish bird clinging to the rail, its tiny feathers blowing every which way.

"I should ask you the same," the bird exclaimed in a bossy little voice. "What on earth are you doing out here?"

Mariah was beyond shock.

"I have an important meeting with a horseshoe crab," she said, thinking how silly it was to be making excuses to a little bird, but the bird commanded respect.

"Meeting with Nelson Telson is canceled due to inclement weather," peeped the bird. "Rescheduled for next sun at low water. Please respond at your earliest convenience...which is now." The bird tapped a tiny talon impatiently.

"Oh, yes, yes! I'll be there for certain," said Mariah. "Next sun at low water."

The little bird took off. "But wait," Mariah called. "I didn't catch your name."

"Peep," said the bird as it darted away under the bridge.

Chapter IV

Ancestors

A beam of sunshine streamed across the wallpaper roses making them pinker than ever. Mariah had a good sleep after soaking in a hot tub before bed. Her mother had been standing at the door waiting for her when she got home.

After breakfast she went to the garage and replaced her bike's inner tube and inflated the tire. Just last month her dad had shown her how to change a flat. Low tide was at 12:15, and she could hardly wait to get out of the house and over the bridge. She decided to go early and collect more shells. She would pack a lunch and bring her beach towel – make a day of it.

"Have you applied sunscreen?" her mother asked, already knowing the answer as she searched through the jumble in a kitchen drawer.

She stood still while her mom smeared sunscreen over her nose and cheeks. "Be sure to wear your hat," she warned, as if going hatless was a matter of life or death. "And the bike helmet, too."

"I will, I promise," said Mariah as she headed

through the mudroom with her lunch and towel.

Thumpity thumpity thumpity thumpity her bike wheels rolled across the bridge. The water was still a bit choppy from the storm, but there was hardly a cloud in the sky. A great blue heron, startled by her approach, flapped its big wings and began its long, labored ascent from the marsh, up and over the water. Mariah stopped to watch. What a miracle, she thought, that such a big bird could even get off the ground, let alone fly with such grace and beauty. Its big gray wings flapped slowly, pushing and pulling on the air. Was it possible that this bird was Aaron the heron with the telson for a beak? It was not facing her, and by then it had flown too high into the sunshine for her to tell.

Leaving her bike in the rack at the edge of the parking lot Mariah skipped down the sandy path to the bay side of the beach. The tide wasn't completely low yet. She reached into her pocket for the spearhead, turning it over and over in her hand, imagining the Indian attaching this stone point to a shaft, winding it with rawhide; she saw him aiming it at a wide-eyed deer.

Mariah pulled off her sneakers, tossed them on her towel, and ran down to the shore to find Nelson. The tops of the rocks where she had met him the first time were just peeking out of the receding water. She saw a couple of horseshoe crabs cruising along in the shallows, but they all had full-length tails. Well, if she found him in the water, she certainly wasn't going to yank him out by the telson.

She walked the edge of the water, one foot in, one foot out, impatient to show off her spearhead. Every few seconds she stopped and inspected it, rubbing her thumb along its shiny surfaces, marveling at the workmanship of its serrated edges and practically perfect point. When she next looked down at her feet, there was Nelson, half in and half out of the water.

"Oh Nelson," she cried with excitement. "Look what I found. It's a spearhead!" She held her open palm down in front of Nelson, and waited for him to say something when it occurred to her that he may not talk at all, and maybe this whole thing was all in her imagination: the crab, the fox, that bossy little bird. The silence of the hard brown animal felt lonelier and emptier than anything she had ever known. *Silly*, she admonished herself as she knelt down and touched the armor-like shell. How had she been so silly to have ever actually believed she had spoken to an old brown horseshoe crab whose ability to talk seemed about as likely as the dark, wet rock that sat motionless in the sand?

"My dear," he began to her great relief, "we horseshoe crabs have ten eyes, but alas, our vision, especially in the daytime, is quite poor. I can detect your shape, but not a small item in your hand."

"It's a spearhead! From the Indians a long time ago."

"Indians?"

"People, natives, here a long time ago."

"Ah," he said. "The People of the First Light, not so long ago, really."

"The People of The First Light," she repeated. This was the second time she had heard that. "What a beautiful name."

"Wampanaog," said Nelson. "They name themselves after the land that sustains them, that flavors the water they drink. What is in the land is in the water, so it is in them. As it is in all of us."

She rubbed the stone between her fingertips. "And so, it was a Person of the First Light who made this?"

"Yes. Is the point of stone or of telson?"

"It's stone, and it's beautiful."

"A weapon of peace," he said.

"Huh?" she said, thinking of cowboy and Indian movies where everybody was shooting each other with guns and bows and arrows.

"You'll find out," he answered mysteriously.

Mariah looked at Nelson's half-telson. "They made spears from telsons, too?"

"Yes, small spears and many other things. Horseshoe crabs have been useful to other creatures throughout history, and we proudly continue our tradition to this day."

"Useful?" Mariah remembered the encyclopedia article about them being ground up for fertilizer; hopefully this wasn't what he was talking about.

"My ancestors roamed these waters 520 million years ago. We horseshoe crabs have seen things come and go in the grand cycles of creation," he said with dramatic flair. "We're 'fifth business' in the great dramas of the earth, always in the background, never starring in a leading role, but many stories could not unfold or conclude without us." Nelson's long, dramatic pause drew Mariah closer.

"Please, go on," she whispered.

"We have been around for ages and ages, and ice ages," he chuckled, "and the story I'm about to tell begins at the end of the most recent ice age, oh, about 15,000 years ago."

Nelson began his story.

When the earth was clean, and men were more like apes, which is to say they had not yet developed all those things that pollute and litter our surroundings, my ancestors roamed the tidal bays and inlets much as they do today. Of course, our sharp tails were just the things for spearing fish and small animals for humans to eat. Why chip away at a piece of stone when the telson is pre-made and ready for use? But the telson doesn't have the weight of stone with the momentum to send a spear a good distance and into the tough hide of a deer, bear, or sloth—or a great woolly

mammoth!

Mariah felt the heaviness of the spearhead in her hand. She touched the hard sharpness of its point, and suddenly saw massive ice sheets bridging watery gaps. She crossed the frozen water with her small pack, roaming in search of food.

The waters were very cold, as was the air. Men were hairy but not hairy enough to stay warm in the chilling frost of an ice age. Those too tired or old, wounded or ill fell by the wayside and died a death that was quiet and peaceful and cold, just like any other creature. Hungry bears, big cats and scavenging birds quickly ate up the remains.

The frigid wind chilled Mariah's back as she limped over hard, gravelly ground scraped bare by the weather. She had fallen behind. Her feet were bound in stiff animal skins that had rubbed her ankle raw. She passed a heap of bones long since picked clean and whitened by the sun, and hurried along to catch up. Ahead of her, the small group wandered on, six in all, two adults and four small children.

The woman had born two sets of twins in as many years. She carried the babies close to her heart, wrapped for warmth in animal hides.

Humans had just figured out how to count, and it was easy for the tired mother to see that she had only two breasts to feed her four hungry children. The elder hunter, father of the father, had recently met his death when the ice floe he was fishing on broke beneath his feet sending him into the cold, briny deep. Now all of the hunting fell upon the young father, and the last time this family had seen a large quantity of food was when they had come upon a wounded ground sloth that was easily slain. The hunter had finished off the beast with a mammoth thighbone club he had found along the way and carried with him everywhere.

They came upon a tidal inlet. The sun warmed the salty water so that just the edges gleamed with ice. She watched as the mother reached into the frigid water for a horseshoe crab, pulled off the legs and sucked the blood and what small flesh there was out of the shell. Mariah was so hungry she did the same. The blood turned blue when it hit the air, and left a coppery taste in her mouth.

The hunter, after he had drained some claws himself, snapped off the telsons from two crabs. He went to the edge of the marsh with a telson in each hand, and squatted there, waiting for a fish to come by. He stabbed wildly at the water, and finally got a fish.

After a while he became quite proficient at spearing fish, so the family stayed put on the hillside near the food source. The mother was happy that the older twins could have fish to eat, but the family was still in great need of animal skins to keep them warm.

As night fell, Mariah huddled with the family in a smelly mass under their sparse collection of animal skins. The skins were stiff and cold around the edges. She pressed closer to the bigger twins, and tucked the skin around her feet.

One time while the father was off in search of a beast to slay, a great woolly mammoth lumbered onto the scene. It was docile and friendly – and warm!

The children climbed on it and snuggled in the folds of its enormous hide. Mariah sat against it, stroking its long hair and thinking what a warm hide this animal would make. But then it occurred to her that the heat-generating mammoth was worth more to the family alive than dead. As she watched the little ones climb on the animal, she noticed that some of the long shaggy hair was coming out and falling to the icy ground. She gathered it up and wrapped it around her sore ankle. She ran her hands down the flank of the beast, and got bunches of the long, soft wool. She gave the wool to the mother.

The young hunter returned with fish to eat, but no large creature of flesh and hide. When he saw the great woolly mammoth he raised his club to bludgeon the beast. The mother stood before him with her arms raised. They didn't have much language, but she made it clear that the animal was providing warmth for the family, and there would be no bludgeoning that day. She showed him the long woolly hair, touched his cheek with it, and then she did something amazing.

Mariah leaned against the warm beast and watched as the mother showed the father how she was creating fabric by using two telsons she had smoothed on a stone. She knitted the long hairs together, clickety click, twisting and knitting, twisting and knitting. The man looked on in awe. Mariah ran her hand down the side of the beast, and brought the mother more wool.

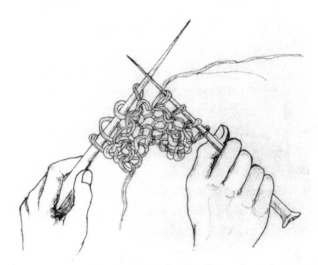

It wasn't long before she had made a long warm wrap for each of the small ones, and a crude hat for the hunter. She made blankets and shawls, and soon the family was rich with warm coverings. She created a fishnet of loosely knitted wool that caught enough fish with one swipe through the water for the family's daily needs. From then on, the hunter had no need to roam very far. The ice was receding, and that family's ancestors thrived along the banks of the tidal inlet for many generations to come.

The mammoth lived a long and happy life as one of the very first domesticated beasts. When it died, the family praised it for its wool and warmth, and the hide it left behind. They also honored the horseshoe crab for the modest gifts it had given them.

"So, you see," said Nelson, "the horseshoe crabs' telsons were not merely used as spears, but also were the world's first knitting needles."

"Wow," she whispered. "Something happened just then when you were telling me that story. You started the telling, and I... I'm not sure how to explain this. I think I slipped into the story!"

She leaned down and whispered to Nelson. "I felt the chilly ice under my feet, and I was shivering in the cold. I smelled the hides and drank horseshoe crab blood. I touched the softness of the mammoth's wool and felt the heat from its body!"

"You were there," he said calmly.

"I really was!" She didn't know if Nelson was serious or kidding, if she had to convince him, or convince herself. "I really was there!"

"Yes, you were."

"But that's impossible!"

"How can you doubt it when you just experienced it?"

"But how? How can it be?" She was confused.

Nelson sighed deeply. "We are the keepers of time."

"You mean, horseshoe crabs?" Mariah's eyes grew wide as she looked at Nelson's sturdy old shell. She remembered something she had read about horseshoe crabs in a *National Geographic* magazine. It said that they have remained changeless throughout time. They were already ancient when the first dinosaurs roamed the planet.

"I think I'm beginning to understand," she said, hopefully. "You are the same now as you were then. You are timeless."

"Time-full," said Nelson, "and so are you."

"Okay, full of time rather than without time; I get it. But that doesn't explain how I was in your story, in another time."

"Another now."

"Another now, then. How did I get there?" All this talk of time was trying her patience.

"Simple, my dear. A wormhole."

Mariah imagined the dark voids of outer space. She wasn't a stranger to science fiction, and she'd heard about wormholes, black holes, and things like that out in space. But she was standing here in the sunshine on a mudflat in Massachusetts! "But, wormholes are supposed to be in outer space."

"This is space. Inner space, outer space, other space, the space between two grains of sand… it's all the same space; it's all the same time—now."

Mariah looked down around her. Busy snails moved slowly along leaving little rivers in the mud. Bits of shells and rocks and seaweed were scattered all about, and thousands of clam holes and wormholes were everywhere she looked.

"You mean a real wormhole? From the worms you

eat? In the mud?" Regular old wormholes just seemed too commonplace for such magic.

"Exactly," said Nelson.

"Unbelievable," said she. But here she was having this discussion with a talking horseshoe crab. Why then couldn't she believe she had actually traveled in time through a wormhole?

In her mind's eye she revisited the story, the family and how they had worked so hard to survive—how if they hadn't survived, maybe there wouldn't be any people at all, just like there weren't any woolly mammoths.

"But what if I had done something back there in the cold time? What if I'd given them a disease or germ or something? Then, might I have changed the course of history? People might not have survived, and I might not have been at all, and then I couldn't have gone there."

"Ah, the paradox," said Nelson. "Is that what you're worried about?"

"Yes, if that's what it is. The paradox."

A motorboat whizzed by full throttle out in the channel. Its wake sent a batch of waves onshore, much bigger and more forceful than the small ones that had been lapping the sand that afternoon. A wave lifted Nelson up and drew him back into the water. Mariah watched as he caught hold of the bottom and used the next wave to bring himself back up to where they had been talking. "Humans," he muttered at the inconvenience, but then caught himself when he remembered to whom he was talking. "Not you." The water had darkened his shell that had begun to dry out in the sun.

"Oh, yes," he continued. " Just then, when you were remembering the story, you were in a now, but you were also in a then, so you were in two nows at once. Yes?"

"I guess so." Mariah drew her big toe over the wet sand, drawing the never ending loops of infinity, around and around, over and over again.

"The word universe gets thrown around a lot, but what we have here is really more of a multi-verse, lots of nows happening all at once."

"But then, what is time? What is the past?"

"Time is relative. The past is evidence of change, nows we remember."

"Relative?" Mariah scratched her head.

"It depends on your relationship to it. Without your clocks to count minutes, it has no point of reference, no start or finish."

The shadows were getting long. Nelson and Mariah had been inching their way toward the dunes as the tide rose. It was nearly time to go home for supper, and she hadn't even eaten her lunch. She hadn't gathered any shells either.

"Oh my goodness! I completely lost track of the time, I mean the nows!" With school starting on Monday, Mariah was anxious about when she might see Nelson again. "I've got to get home. Can we make a plan to meet soon?"

"Let us allow chance, the best maker of opportunities, to create our schedule for us, shall we?"

Mariah wasn't too keen on that idea, but she was willing to go along. "Okay. I don't think I can come tomorrow anyway. Is this the place I will find you?"

"You may find me here or nearby in these waters. Sometimes I end up on the other side."

"The other side! Not the ocean. I'd never find you."

"No, no, the other side of the bay. The northeast weather sometimes takes me there. It's quite pleasant over there."

"Yes, it is," Mariah agreed, imagining Nelson crawling along amongst the eel grass of the little beach at the end of her lane. She held her spearhead tightly in her hand, and looked down the shoreline wistfully. She would say goodbye without being sad or nervous that she might never see him again. A couple of sandpipers darted along the edge of the water. They looked like the bird she had met the day before.

"Nelson," she said. "Who was the little bird that met me on the bridge yesterday? I tried to get her name but she flew away too quickly."

"Oh, that was a Peep."

"A Peep?"

"They're all Peeps."

"It was good of her to meet me on the bridge, but she sure was bossy."

"Those Peeps are all business, but they're never too busy to do a favor for a someone else. Remember how they helped Aaron with his beak? I had asked them to do that. Very helpful birds, those Peeps. They don't live here; they're just passing through, going southward now. They are beholden to us for the sustenance they need when they are traveling north to breed in the spring. If it weren't for us horseshoe crabs, those birds would never have enough energy to finish the trip, and that would be the end of them. No nesting, no breeding, no re-Peeps."

Mariah giggled. "What do you mean by sustenance?"

Nelson told her that female horseshoe crabs lay thousands of eggs each time they mate during the spring and summer. They bury the eggs in nests in the sand at high tide during the full and new moons. The eggs are rich with protein and nutrients, a perfect food for hungry shorebirds on a long trip. The Peeps time their northward migration so they arrive along certain shores just after the horseshoe crabs have laid their eggs.

"But, how do they know?"

"How do you know to wake up in the morning? How do we know to spawn on the summer tide when the moon is full? Those answers are not known; they are felt. They just *are*. "

You are not going to believe this but I talked to Nelson the horseshoe crab today and he told me a lot about horseshoe crabs. If it weren't for horseshoe crabs, those little sandpipers, the Peeps, wouldn't exist! They eat horseshoe crab eggs on their way north to nest and lay their own eggs.

I also went to another now in the ice age through a WORMHOLE, a real wormhole from a sea worm. I thought wormholes were up in space but Nelson said that everything is in space so this regular wormhole was in space too. I was with a family. It was real cold and I drank the blood of a horseshoe crab. It was blue and tasted like copper. If it weren't for those horseshoe crabs those people wouldn't have been able to survive. I touched a wooly mammoth and the mother made knitted things from the wool using horseshoe crab tails – TELSONS – for knitting needles. I am not kidding. I think my spearhead is magic.

Chapter V

Room 6B

It was still dark when Mariah woke up to the shrill ringing of her new alarm clock. Her mother had handed it to her the night before saying that it was the loudest alarm clock money can buy, and there would be no excuses for missing the bus. She reached out into the morning air and pressed the snooze button, pulled her pillow over her head and snuggled deeply. Nelson's words came to her. *How do you know to wake up in the morning?* If not for school and the loudest alarm clock money can buy, she would be waking up with the sun, with the birds, that is how.

When the clock rang again, she peeked out from under her pillow to find the wallpaper roses bathed in the real rosy light of day. She dragged herself from the warm bed. Bed rhymes with dread, she said to herself, and dread is what she felt at the thought of the first day of school.

Dressed and ready with her new backpack slung over her shoulder, Mariah headed up the lane to the bus stop. On her way out the door her mother had kissed her on the forehead, wished her lots of luck, and along with enough lunch money for the week, handed her the welcoming letter from the principal that included her class assignment: Room 6B, Mrs. Tarbox.

Stepping out into the lane, she couldn't help but notice what a perfectly perfect day it was. A praying mantis stood, swaying like a loose twig in a patch of sunlight on the front steps waiting for an unsuspecting bug to come by. Birds called from the treetops, and crickets chirped in the stone wall. Why did school have to start when the air was so warm and soft? There were three more weeks left of actual summer before autumn.

She turned around and faced the bright patch of sparkling water down at the end of the lane. A large black and white bird seemed to stand still in the sky, beating its big wings over the water. Then, all in one motion, the bird plunged down like a rocket, landed feet first, and with a splash pulled itself up and out of the bay clutching a fish that was nearly as big as it was. The bird slowly gained altitude as it flew up the lane toward her. Mariah was awestruck. How could that bird be strong enough to hold onto that big fish and stay in the air? The dripping fish flopped and arched in its grasp as the bird pumped its wings in a forceful, lopsided rhythm. As it flew near, a drop of cold, salty water splashed onto Mariah's cheek, and the bird looked down at her. Its sharp gaze made her heart leap, and right then she realized that she was an animal too, just like that bird.

Gaining momentum, the bird flew low and parallel with the land, following the lane as if it were an uphill river. Off it went with its struggling prey, up over Washington Street to Western Way and out of sight. Mariah caught her breath, her eyes widened, and a smile crept over her face.

The light salty breeze filled her with longing. Yes, she was an animal too, and she wanted to be outside on this beautiful day. She wished she were a bird or a fish, well, maybe not a fish—a gull, or a cat, or a horseshoe crab—anything but a human kid who had to face sixth grade in another new school. The approaching bus rumbled louder. She ran up to meet it just as it squeaked to a stop at the top of Winsor Street, the street that was really a lane.

The noise of kids talking and squirming on the bus was overwhelming. The smell of diesel fumes, kid sweat and upholstery made her want to hold her breath. She found an empty seat near the front, sat down and covered her ears while pretending to read the class assignment letter in her lap. The bus bounced along Washington Street, down Powder Point Avenue to the bridge, and up King Caesar Road, stopping often to pick up more kids.

Each time it stopped she hoped no one would sit down next to her, but the bus was filling up and she felt the inevitable tap on her shoulder. She glanced up to find a friendly brown face, very dark and different from all of the other faces on the bus. Mariah slid over so he could sit down. She was relieved that he didn't talk to her, and when they got to school his quiet smile thanked her for sharing the seat.

The kids in Room 6B were rowdy and full of summer spunk. Mariah stood in the doorway looking around for an empty desk but every seat was taken. She'd just have to stand there until the teacher came. A spitball flew past her and landed on the blackboard. A small cluster of kids at the back of the room laughed and whispered. One of the kids glanced up at her. Were they laughing at her?

Just then someone bumped her from behind, knocking her forward into the room where her arm caught the first desk sending a neat pile of textbooks crashing to the floor. The pretty blonde girl who was sitting there clicked her tongue, rolled her eyes, and sighed at Mariah's clumsiness. Before she had a chance to say excuse me and turn around, a voice bellowed, "Clear the exit! Take your seat! All pupils are to be seated immediately upon entering my room."

Mariah turned to explain, "But..." and was cut off abruptly.

"Don't 'but' me, missy. Take your seat!"

Mariah stood there holding the class assignment letter. No empty seats had miraculously appeared. All the kids were watching her, and her cheeks began to burn. She turned to Mrs. Tarbox. The woman had a huge face with large jowls, beefy lips, and a broad nose with big flaring nostrils. She glared at Mariah.

Mrs. Tarbox snatched the letter from Mariah's hand and adjusted her glasses. She mumbled while she read. "Humph, that makes twenty-seven. This class is already overcrowded. Go find the janitor and have him bring a desk."

Mariah did as she was told. It was a relief to wander the quiet, empty halls, past the classroom doors where she could hear teaching going on. She wandered the halls for quite some time before she found the janitor. He got an extra desk from the storeroom. As they approached the door to her classroom, the janitor got a knowing look on his face. "Mrs. Tarbox, huh?" Mariah nodded. "Good luck, kid," he whispered as they entered the room.

"Put it over there," said Mrs. Tarbox, interrupting the blonde girl who was standing by her desk. She pointed to the far side of the classroom that was lined with tall, wide windows.

Mariah's desk was placed off to the side of the fifth row. She sat down and tried to pay attention. In the big maple tree outside, two squirrels chased each other back and forth, up and down, around and around. There was hardly a cloud in the sky. A red-tail hawk sailed high over the marsh to the north. As she watched it she thought about the time she called one a rafter, since it coasted so high up in the sky as if it were in the rafters. Her mother had corrected her, "Raptor," she'd said, "r-a-p-t-o-r," telling her to look it up in the dictionary. Mariah was surprised to find that it meant ravager and plunderer—hardly a fair way to describe a beautiful bird of prey like the one she had seen that morning working so hard to hold onto that fish.

"...and that some people are two-faced, and can't be trusted," said the blonde girl near the doorway, nodding her head, tossing her hair affectedly, and sitting down. Mrs. Tarbox pointed at one of the boys at the back of the room. "Jonathan," she snapped, "stand up and address the class."

The boy was handsome and very grown up for his age. Tanned and confident in his clean oxford shirt, he got up and took on the stance of a fashion model. He didn't seem the least bit intimidated by Mrs. Tarbox. "This summer we did the usual: cruised from Bar Harbor to Buzzards Bay, sailed a lot, and stayed at my grandparents' on the Vineyard." Mariah heard his voice droning on about yacht clubs and regattas and tennis matches. She perked up when she heard him say, "Sometimes it's okay to lie."

What's this all about, she thought as she watched a couple of sparrows hop around on the sidewalk outside the window.

"Expatiate," said Mrs. Tarbox.

"Huh?" said the boy.

"Elaborate. Tell us more."

"My mom asked my step-dad if she looked fat in this dress, and he said, 'No, you look beautiful.' But she really did look fat, and I said so, and she got all mad and cried, and my step-dad said my mom always looks beautiful to him, and sometimes it's better to tell a small lie than hurt someone's feelings." Some of the kids laughed.

Mrs. Tarbox dismissed him with a nod. "All right, that's just about everyone, except..." She scanned the room. Mariah's heart began to thump, thump, thump, higher and higher in her chest as she faced the fact that the teacher's eyes had landed on her. Mrs. Tarbox raised her eyebrows higher, and when Mariah didn't respond quickly enough, she squinted at the class assignment letter and roared, "Miss Miller, Mayreeha Miller! Address the class."

Mariah was baffled; she wasn't sure what Mrs. Tarbox wanted. She had half-heard what the boy had said, but she was confused. Her heart was pounding, and the blood was rushing through her ears so she could hardly hear. She stood up beside her desk, and tried to find her voice. "Ma-rye-ah," she corrected the teacher's pronunciation.

"Speak up!" said Mrs. Tarbox.

Mariah looked at the floor and summoned the courage to speak again. Her heart hammered harder. Mrs. Tarbox was losing patience.

"Speak up," she repeated, coming out from behind her desk and standing a few feet in front of Mariah.

Mariah repeated her name louder, and Mrs. Tarbox told her again to address the class. But Mariah didn't know what she was supposed to talk about; she hadn't heard the assignment; she had been out in the quiet halls looking for the janitor. Her timid gaze remained on the floor. She felt the heat of Mrs. Tarbox just before the toes of her sensible shoes came into view. "Address the class," said Mrs. Tarbox.

Her heart beat in syncopated time, thump by trembling thump, as she stood waiting for a miracle. There was nothing to say until she knew what to say. What could she say?

"ADDRESS THE CLASS!" Mrs. Tarbox's breath scorched Mariah's face.

She heard a whispering behind her, "Briefly summarize your summer, and tell about a lesson you learned."

Okay, now that she knew what it was she was supposed to do, she could at least try to get it over with so she could sit down. She felt the entire class watching her and waiting. Mrs. Tarbox stood impatiently with her hands on her big hips. Mariah's head was throbbing. She took a deep breath. "Well," she began, "we…"

Mrs. Tarbox cut her short, "We drink from a well; we don't begin a sentence with one!"

Mariah was stunned. "Well," she began again, only to be stopped again.

Mrs. Tarbox roared, "Did I ask you how you are feeling? No, I did not!" Her shoes came a few inches closer, squarely into Mariah's line of sight. They looked like nurses' shoes, but they were scuffed and black.

Mariah opened her mouth to begin again.

"Look up when you are speaking!" The sharp words cut like a knife.

Mariah fought back angry tears. A hushed silence fell over the classroom. Looking up, she searched Mrs. Tarbox's face for a hint of encouragement but found none. She took a few deep breaths, pleading with her heart to stop pounding. "This summer we moved here from Pennsylvania," she said relaxing a little bit and looking down again. But before she knew what was happening, Mrs. Tarbox cut in again.

"Head up," she commanded.

Mariah looked straight ahead at Mrs. Tarbox's thick neck, for she could not bring herself to meet her unkind eyes. On that big neck was a large mole with group of gray hairs sprouting from the center. Time stood still. Mariah thought about Nelson and what they talked about after she had been in the ice age, about time being lots of nows, always present. This was one now she would gladly trade for another.

"My dad grew up here…"

"Hmm," said Mrs. Tarbox, as though she now understood everything. "Joseph Miller?" she said, as if she were speaking the name of the devil.

"He's my uncle," said Mariah.

"Speak up," said Mrs. Tarbox. Mariah repeated herself, and then stood there silently.

"The lesson," whispered the voice behind her.

She had learned a lot of lessons that summer, but she couldn't think of anything to say. All she could think about was how cruel Mrs. Tarbox was, and how she wished she could disappear from this classroom. She started to look down, but caught herself before she might have been corrected again.

She remembered something her mother had said after an unpleasant experience with a sales clerk. "You can catch more flies with honey than with vinegar," she blurted out.

Mrs. Tarbox feigned ignorance. "And exactly what does that mean?"

"That kindness is more attractive than meanness."

Mariah raised her eyes to Mrs. Tarbox's.

The teacher turned back to go to her desk at the front of the room. "Thank you. Be seated," she mumbled.

Mariah snuck a peek at the owner of the helpful little voice. It was the dark, quiet boy from the bus. She hadn't noticed him earlier when she had entered the room, but she sure was glad to see him now. "Thanks," she whispered.

On the bus ride home Mariah and the boy shared a seat. They sat quietly, and when the bus reached his stop, he said, "See you tomorrow." She smiled back, all the while wishing tomorrow did not have to include Mrs. Tarbox.

As soon as she got home and checked in with her mother, she changed her clothes, slipped her spearhead into her pocket, hopped on her bike, and rode up Washington Street. The wind on her face was a welcome change from the stuffy classroom and smelly school bus. Free as a bird, she coasted down the hill and through Snug Harbor. She went over the Bluefish Bridge and past the flagpole. When she got to the fork in the road, she stopped and looked at the street signs. To her left was Powder Point Avenue, the route her mom took to the beach, and to her right was King Caesar Road. Her bus had gone down Powder Point and up King Caesar. She chose King Caesar hoping she might see the boy from the bus. There was no sign of him anywhere near his stop, so she pedaled onward to the bridge. Maybe she would see Nelson.

She had just about reached the other side of the bridge when the great blue heron flapped its big wings and took off. This time, though, she saw his beak, and if she was not mistaken, it looked like it could have been a telson.

"Aaron!" she called, "Is that you?" The big bird didn't seem to hear her as he flew further and further away across the Back River.

Mariah felt lonelier than ever. The tide wasn't low, and she probably wouldn't find Nelson. Aaron, if it was Aaron, had ignored her. She hated her new school. She hated her new teacher. She trudged over the path through the dunes to the ocean side, and looked out at the broad blue horizon.

How many times had they moved in her eleven years, from places she had only heard about before she could remember? She knew she had lived in Washington, DC and Chicago but she couldn't remember either one. And then there was New York, and then Virginia, Maine, Connecticut, Pennsylvania, and now Massachusetts. Six different states, six different towns, six grades in six different schools, six different lives. And each time she had had to start all over again. Who was she going to be now? There were the studious types, the jokers, the athletes, the popular kids. Where did she fit in? Nowhere. She never stayed anywhere long enough. It seemed easier just to not bother trying to make any friends at all.

She just could not help being shy. Whenever she had to get up in front of the class her heart pounded so wildly she thought she was going to die. Now, just thinking about appearing in school again after being so embarrassed by Mrs. Tarbox made her feel shaky all over. Tears filled her eyes.

Looking out past the horizon, she thought about how small and stupid all of this seemed compared to the bigness of the ocean and the vastness of the universe. She sat down in the white sand, pulled her spearhead from her pocket, and wrapped her arms around her knees. The stone was familiar in her hand. The soothing sound of the ocean waves entered her ears, rolling and receding, rolling and receding, rocking her in the arms of Mother Earth.

The sound of the sea was all she heard or felt. Something was happening; she was slipping, slipping away into a green watery world. She felt the water rise up around her. Was this another now? She was swimming, not like a person, but like some sea animal. It felt like a dream, but she had never dreamt of being undersea before. She swam and swam, navigating mazes of suspended litter, dodging gigantic fishing nets, plastic bags, and sunken pools of toxic smelling, heavy black oil that she knew could suffocate her if she came too close. It was all human junk; no other animal of the earth could have done this. The loud humming and whining of engines and propellers passed through the water, stabbing her ears and making her lose her sense of direction and purpose. *Why was she here?*

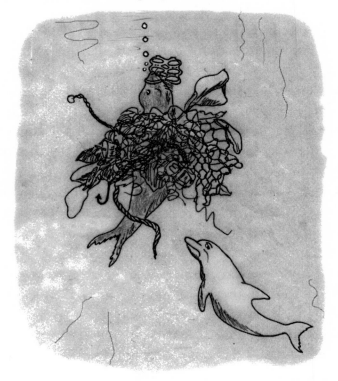

Near the surface she saw a mass of debris wiggling and writhing. She swam closer to find a creature bobbing and jerking, trying to untangle itself but getting more and more tangled instead. She heard its strangled cries for help. Whatever it was, it was drowning, and she raced to set it free. As she set to work Mariah realized that she had no hands or feet, only a tail and flippers. She was a sea creature, what kind, she did not know. But she had to act fast, so she pushed her snout up into the tangle of trash, prying loose the cocoon of snarled fishing line.

As she struggled with the slimy mess, a motorboat's churning propeller came frighteningly close to her back, its wake knocking her about and upsetting the small progress she had made. Couldn't they see? Didn't they care? Why did they have to go so fast?

With the sharpness of her teeth and the power of her will, she finally tore away enough of the tangle to reveal a silky brown seal whose round eyes looked out from beneath a shroud of seaweed and plastic litter. Tiny air bubbles streamed from its muzzle, which was snared in a plastic loop that once held a beer can. Mariah grasped a loop with her teeth and pulled hard. Once free, the seal shook away the remaining bits of slime and seaweed, and showed its appreciation by chirping with glee and turning happy corkscrews through the water.

Mariah was glad she had been able to help, so happy in fact, she dipped and twisted, gliding through the water, and turned a few corkscrews herself.

As she swam along, she noticed that the water was becoming cleaner and bluer. The sound of engines faded.   She encountered less and less debris and growth, and more and more clear water and schools of fish. Billowing underwater clouds of shrimp and other small, shiny creatures changed direction when she swam near. The light glimmered in new patterns as all the tiny bodies darted and moved as one.

She did not know what kind of animal she was, but she was becoming so comfortable gliding along in the sea that she really didn't care. Now she could hear the true sounds of the deep, and this was real music. Long and low, deep bass songs lay under piping melodies that weaved through the water. The rhythm of this music was the rhythm of the sea, and Mariah's sleek sea body danced through the water. She began to feel so free and exhilarated that, just for the joy of it, she wiggled her tail up and down, and leapt up out of the water and into the bright blue sky! Arching her body, she turned gracefully and slipped back into the watery depths.

She realized she was not alone.   Several other creatures swam with her, each singing harmonious parts of the same song, and following her every move. They looked like small whales, but not quite like whales, and not quite like dolphins either.   Their golden skin shimmered in the dappled light as they moved through the water. Their voices were golden, too, and as they sang higher and higher to a crescendo, one or two flew up through the surface, arched and dove back in just as she had.

Singing and leaping, she moved along with her pod to the south. They came around the Gurnet, and then swam past Clark's Island, and into the warmer water of the bay. Clark's Island was attached to Saquish, and not an island at all, just a giant rock sticking up out of the water. When she leapt up into the air again, she realized that there were no traces of man: no houses or boats or lobster traps or buoys. It was just the creatures of the sea and she, and the fresh smells of pristine water and air.

The music of the bay, made by millions of animals much smaller than those of the deep, was higher and sweeter. The bowl shape of the bay helped the sounds swirl and mix with each other. She heard the songs of snails and barnacles and mussels and clams. The barnacles, their legs waving in the currents thrummed like the string section of this incredible orchestra. She thought about those tiny shells she had found on the day she met Nelson and heard the tinkling music they made. And then she heard a sound she recognized. It was a deep and thoughtful droning sound, like a cheerful old man humming. She swam along in the warm water of the peninsula's inside shore until she found him.

"Oh Nelson," she cried, "I'm so happy to see you here!"

As suddenly as she had slipped into the deep, now she found herself bone dry, on land, on the bay side of the big beach, sitting on a rock, talking to Nelson.

"How did I get over here?"

"You swam, my dear."

"I know I was swimming, but how did that happen? One minute I'm sitting over there," she pointed to the ocean side, "and then I'm some sea animal. And now, here I am completely dry and over here!" Mariah was waving her arms around pointing here and there. She looked at her hand, turned her palm up to reveal the spearhead, and wiggled her fingers, admiring them. "These certainly are handy!" she laughed. "I think I started in a forward now – which wasn't so nice. Then I went backwards in time, and it was beautiful. But how? Was there a wormhole in the sand?"

"Oh, no. Wormholes aren't the only ways to get around. You went by slipstream."

"Slipstream?"

"Yes, much like a wormhole, but the space through which you travel is between water molecules. Your tears became the passage to a sea of nows."

Mariah's eyes were wide with amazement. "Oh, so that's why I didn't just land in a different now. It was as though I swam from one now to another and then another."

"That you did, my dear. You slipped through the streamtime."

"Slipped through the streamtime," Mariah repeated dreamily, "I really like the sound of that." It made her think of the beautiful music she had heard, the songs of the sea and the sweet symphony of the bay. "Everything, the water and sky, it was all so blue. When I leapt out of the water, everything was so clear!"

"And for a very good reason."

Mariah remembered the mess she had seen and smelled when she was helping untangle the seal. "Because there were no people around to pollute things yet?"

"That, and something much more important," said Nelson. He seemed to be thinking very hard about what he was about to say. Mariah waited. A big loud jet soaring high overhead drowned out the sound of the waves on the ocean side.

When it was quiet again Nelson spoke. "Because your voice is as clear as that sky, and your truth is true blue."

She was so tired after dinner, she almost forgot to write in her journal. But there was so much to say, she reached into her nightstand and brought it out.

I hate my new school. I hate Mrs. Tarbox. She is a mean old bat. Maybe I can get the chicken pox or something so I don't have to go to school tomorrow. I went to the beach and turned into a dolphin or something and swam through time. I saved a seal that was all tangled up in litter and stuff. He was drowning, but he's okay now. Nelson says I slipped through the streamtime! The music in the water was really nice, like magic music. The sea had a deep song and the bay had a high symphony of sounds. I heard Nelson's song, too. Maybe it's all just my imagination, but it seems like it really happened. Like Nelson said, Clear as the sky and true blue. I like him a lot.

I met a nice kid. Don't even know his name, but he's quiet and nice and maybe he'll be my friend. Goodnight.

Chapter VI
Turkey & Heron

School dragged on day after day. Mariah always shared a seat on the bus with the quiet boy whose name was Kip. She was doing her best to stay invisible in the classroom so Mrs. Tarbox wouldn't call on her. She kept to herself and spent most of her time gazing out the window and drawing pictures. She drew pictures of Nelson upside down, Nelson right side up, tiny horseshoe crabs all in a row, herons, seashells, or whatever she had her mind on at the time. She kept the picture she was drawing in the book the class was using, and when Mrs. Tarbox came near her desk Mariah casually flipped the page over as if she were reading.

She was drawing a picture of Mrs. Tarbox during Social Studies. It wasn't a very flattering likeness, but then no likeness of Mrs. Tarbox would be. Mariah was sketching away, wondering what kind of a man would have married such a big meany, and pitying poor Mr. Tarbox whoever he was, when her model came walking toward her desk demanding the answer to some question about rivers and the ancient civilization of Mesopotamia. Mariah had been in a parallel now, in the room but somewhere else, and hardly listening. As she re-entered Mrs. Tarbox's now, Mariah realized that she had not heard the question; she had only heard the words "rivers" and "Mesopotamia".

Remembering the names from the map she had seen in the book, she quickly answered, "Euphrates and Tigris."

"I did not ask you to name the rivers, Miss Miller, I asked you why the people lived in the location between the rivers."

Mariah thought fast. "Be... be... because the soil was good for growing things and the rivers were good for transportation." In her hurry to appease Mrs. Tarbox, she had forgotten to hide her sketch.

Her heart dropped to her feet when she looked up

to see the teacher standing over her and peering down at the portrait.

Before she could flip the page, the big hand of Mrs. Tarbox reached down and snatched up the drawing. Mariah cringed and held her breath, waited for the consequences—the wrath of Mrs. Tarbox, and detention for sure. The whole class waited, too. To the surprise of everyone, Mrs. Tarbox just turned away silently and walked back to her desk. To the class's further amazement, the teacher put the picture carefully into a drawer and continued with the lesson.

The weather was getting crisper as October turned to November. The maple tree in the courtyard outside the classroom window, afire with orange, red, and yellow leaves, called to her under the wide blue sky. All day long Mariah waited until the last bell rang so she could get home and go outside, ride her bike to the big beach or walk down to the bay at the end of the lane.

Now, often when she looked up at the sky, she remembered what Nelson had said, and a small but strong voice deep within her center repeated, *clear as the sky and true blue.* And when she spoke these words inside, she would breathe deeply and pull herself together, standing a little taller and straighter.

"Look at you! Mariah, you're growing like a

beanstalk!" Uncle Joe said when she answered the front door that her mom had decorated for Thanksgiving with a bunch of colorful Indian corn attached to the brass knocker. Stepping back, Uncle Joe pushed her cousin Travis through the door and then held them both shoulder to shoulder, comparing. "Why, you're almost taller than Travis!"

She cringed at the sound of his name, and edged away so her shoulder wouldn't touch his. The last time she had seen her pudgy, mean cousin was the Fourth of July a couple of years ago in Connecticut. Over the course of that weekend he had exploded a toad with a firecracker, poked a garter snake to death with a stick, stuck his chewing gum in her hair, and harassed her old cat Samantha so she hadn't come home for two days. And when he wasn't torturing animals, he was torturing humans such as his younger cousin whenever he got the chance. Mariah was forced to play with him whenever the families got together.

She looked beyond Uncle Joe and Travis, hoping to see her Aunt Cheryl coming up the steps. All Mariah saw was the open trunk of the car with some large suitcases, a TV, and an overflowing laundry bag in it. Uncle Joe looked back, knowing Mariah's next words. "Where's Aunt Cheryl?"

"Oh, honey, didn't they tell you?" Uncle Joe looked sad. His face fidgeted for the right words. "We got a divorce, and Aunt Cheryl has left the family."

Travis looked at his feet. Mariah didn't know what

to say. The warm smell of roasting turkey reminded them of why they were there.

Mariah had set the table with the fancy silverware and plates. She stood back admiring her centerpiece, a bouquet of oak leaves, bittersweet and goldenrod, the last colors of fall. She had made special place cards for each guest, with a picture of an animal drawn on each one. Her mom's had a sandpiper, her dad's had an osprey, Uncle Joe's had a herring gull, and Travis got a funny-looking turkey. Mariah had drawn her favorite bird, the great blue heron, on hers. Now she had to rearrange the places, now that Aunt Cheryl wasn't going to be sitting next to her. Aunt Cheryl's place card had a snowy egret like the ones she always saw out on the marsh. She picked it up off the table and slipped it into her pocket just as her mother was bringing in the serving dishes.

"Why didn't you tell me about the divorce, mom?"

"Well, honey, we didn't want to upset you," said her mother, smiling at Uncle Joe and Travis as they came into the dining room.

The house was filled with the smells of Thanksgiving. Steam rose from the big brown turkey, and Mariah imagined it alive and walking around in the wire enclosure at the turkey farm. All of a sudden she wasn't so hungry.

Her dad sat at the head of the table, but he pushed the turkey towards Uncle Joe to carve. Mariah sat down at her place across from Travis and Uncle Joe. She admired her bouquet and how it brought the happy fall colors inside the house. She glanced over at Travis. His face was pasty and pimply, and he needed a haircut. He was playing a hand-held video game. It kept making small peeping noises like an electronic toad.

"How's school?" asked Uncle Joe.

"Not so good," she said. "I have this mean teacher, Mrs. Tarbox."

"Ha!" said Uncle Joe, "Old Tarbox, eh? She seemed old when I had her. She must be ancient by now." He laughed. "Don't let her get to you, honey. She was actually one of the best teachers I ever had."

Mariah wasn't sure that they were talking about the same person.

Now that they were all seated, her mom said, "This being Thanksgiving, I think we should each say what we are thankful for. I, for one, am thankful for all of the abundance we enjoy and share, our warm house, and all of this yummy food we are about to eat!" She looked across the table at Mariah's dad and raised her eyebrows. "Mike?"

Mariah's father thought for a moment, and said, "I'm thankful for my wonderful family, and my good health." He turned to his brother.

Uncle Joe cleared his throat, and spoke quietly. "I'm thankful that I am here with you today, the people I love. It's been a hard time, but, with your help, we'll get through it." He seemed as though he might cry if he had to say any more words.

All the while Mariah was thinking of all the things she was grateful for: her animal friends, sailing the *Kite*, the warm sun on her face, the stars twinkling at night, the peeps darting along the water's edge, the osprey, Nelson...

Knowing it was his turn, Travis looked up from his video game and shrugged. "I dunno," he said, and started sneezing uncontrollably.

Travis sneezed one sneeze after another with barely a breath in between. Mariah's mother said, "Cover your mouth, dear." But Travis just kept sneezing and sneezing.

Uncle Joe stood up and grabbed Mariah's beautiful centerpiece from the table. "Ah ha! Here's the culprit," he said smiling as though he were a detective who just solved a crime. Carrying the vase of leaves and flowers out to the mudroom, he called back, "Travis has had terrible allergies lately."

Travis sneezed and sneezed. He dropped his video game and held his hands over his face. Mariah looked at the empty spot in the center of the table where her decoration had been, and it seemed as though, along with the bright orange and yellow, happiness had left the room. Mrs. Miller jumped up from her chair, ran into the kitchen, and dashed back with a tissue for him. The sneezing finally stopped, but no one bothered to ask Mariah what she was thankful for. Everyone had forgotten all about it.

Halfway through the meal Uncle Joe said, "After dinner I'll get Travis's things so he can set up camp. I can't tell you how much this means to me."

"I've got the guest room all ready for him." Mariah's mom said cheerfully.

Mariah's eyes widened. She couldn't believe what she was hearing. "What?"

"Oh, Travis is going to be staying with us for a few months."

"Months?"

"Yes, honey, he'll be finishing up the school year here."

"Why?"

"Don't ask so many questions," her mother answered quickly, all the while smiling at Uncle Joe and Travis.

Mariah looked over at Travis. His face was expressionless as he shoveled food into his mouth.

"May I be excused?" Mariah started to leave the table.

"But you haven't finished your dinner. Don't you want dessert? I made your favorite, pumpkin pie."

"That's okay, Mom. I'm really full. I'll have dessert later." Mariah took off out the mudroom door as fast as she could, looking back now and then to make sure Travis wasn't following.

She ran down to the end of the lane. It was warm for November, and having left the house without a sweater, she was glad of it. The tide was dead low. A few egrets waded far off along the edge of the mudflats, and hungry gulls dropped mussels from high up in the air onto the rocks. A group of gulls squabbled over the food. There are laughing gulls and crying gulls, but these were definitely bickering gulls.

She always carried the spearhead with her, except to school, and often reached into her pocket to make sure it was there. It was her touchstone, this object she knew so well, always handy in her pocket. Her mom called it a worry stone when she saw Mariah rolling it around between her fingers, but Mariah felt it was more of a now stone. She pushed it back down to the bottom of her pocket for safety, and walked further out to where the rocks gave way to the mud. The mud was lively with the popping and creaking of millions of clams and worms and mussels and periwinkles. Clam holes squirted as she stepped. All the teeming life around her made her feel more alive than ever. She took a deep breath and smelled the good smell of low tide, of so many things living and dying and decomposing and being born.

Something hit her on the back, and then something hit her leg. A small rock passed by her and landed in the mud. Mariah turned to find Travis armed with a handful of driveway gravel, and on the attack.

"P.U.! It sure stinks around here. Smells like farts." To make his point, he stuck out his tongue and made huge farting noises.

"Smells good to me," Mariah said taking in a big, exaggerated breath like a connoisseur smelling a fine wine. "Ummm, marsh gas!" She loved liking something Travis found offensive.

Travis moved closer, throwing the rocks a little bit harder each time.

"Travis," she yelled. "Why do you have to be so mean?" A pebble whizzed by her ear and splashed into a tidal pool.

"I dunno," he said, grinning maliciously as he chucked another rock at her.

Mariah looked around to find something to throw back at him. She felt a sharp sting on the back of her head, and then another. Hunching down to deflect the onslaught, she reached out to keep from losing her balance. The mud presented itself.

Travis advanced, and as he did each rock hurt more. Mariah didn't give it a second thought as she stretched her fingers wide and dug in deep to fill her two hands with big globs of cold, slimy mud. She wasn't a very good aim, but by now he was at close range.

She turned quickly, and before Travis had a chance to think, she flung the mud at him as hard as she could. One glob hit him on the side of his face, and the other squarely on the bare skin at his open collar.

Mariah watched the big shiny gray glob slide down his chest inside his brand new white dress shirt. Travis was stunned.

"I'm telling," he snorted as he turned and stomped up the path to the lane while Mariah imagined the cold mud running down his belly and hopefully into his pants.

Now what was she going to do? She certainly wasn't about to go home. She looked out at the gray stillness of low tide. The gases rising up from the mud shimmered in the light breeze. She pictured Travis and the mud and began to giggle. The giggle turned to laughter, and the laughter filled the cool air, rolling and tumbling in the space where the water is at high tide. Now, instead of water, a tide of laughter rose up.

She wiped her hands on her dress, and reached into her pocket. The spearhead was warm on her mud-chilled fingers. Silver reflections rippled on the surface of the tidal pool. And as she stood at the edge of that pool gazing at her own smiling reflection, a beautiful heron appeared beside her. It wasn't Aaron the great blue heron. This heron had a perfect heron beak, not a telson. He opened that long, sleek beak and said, "Hi, you must be Mariah."

Flabbergasted to hear this familiar greeting, Mariah's jaw dropped, her cheeks sore from laughing.

"I am Lloyd, son of Aaron The Great."

"So," she giggled, "you must be Lloyd The Great." And just saying that sent her off again into uncontrollable laughter.

"That is true: Great and Blue!" He stood tall and proud.

Mariah nodded, trying to catch her breath. "Where's your father, Aaron the Great?"

"Aaron the Great is late," said Lloyd.

"Oh, is he coming, too?"

"No my dear, he is the late Aaron the Great, and I am his son."

"Wait a minute," said Mariah, "are you saying he's dead?"

"Dead indeed," answered Lloyd matter-of-factly, nodding his long beak up and down. "Expired."

"Aren't you sad?"

"Why be sad? Dying is as much as part of living as being born. Everybody does it; it's inevitable. He was a good old bird, and his time had come. He got tangled up in a bunch of castoff fishing line; thought it was fish. If his eyesight had been better he wouldn't have made that fatal error. I'm here now," he said, "at your service."

Mariah was confused. Lloyd didn't seem angry or sad. And he was right about dying. Every living thing does it. The world depends on it. Why do humans make such a big deal of it?

"I really wanted to meet him," she said. "I'd heard so much about him."

"What am I," squawked Lloyd cocking his head and giving her a sidelong look, "Chopped liver?"

Mariah started to apologize.

"I hear you've been asking a lot of questions about us animals. So, you're curious, eh?"

She nodded. Lloyd got a serious look in his eye, and warned her, "Do you know what mussels do when you ask too many questions?" He didn't wait for her reply. "They clam up!" He pranced about on his spindly legs and rattled his beak like a drum roll.

The bickering gulls started laughing, and Mariah

did too. Now that he had an audience, Lloyd blinked a few times and said, "Two seagulls are flying over a parking lot. One says, "Have you seen the new model Jeep?" The other says, 'Yeah, I just spotted one!'" The gulls swirled around filling the sky with raucous laughter.

It took Mariah a couple of seconds to get the joke, remembering the white spots of gull poop on their windshield. "Bathroom humor," she chuckled as Lloyd squawked and hooted, clacking his beak and snaking his neck every which way.

The tide of laughter rose higher. The lightness in the air made her feel very light, too, as if her feet were hardly touching the ground.

"Hop on," said the bird.

She had had enough bizarre experiences lately, so she didn't ask any questions. And just as she was thinking, *but how can I hop on?*, either she got smaller or Lloyd got bigger, or maybe a bit of both, and suddenly she was in the soft feathers between Lloyd's great wings. The tips of those wings nearly brushed the mud as he stepped forward on his long legs, into the wind, stepping and flapping, stepping and flapping, taking off into the air. Mariah clung to the big bird's neck to keep from falling off as his body rose and fell with each enormous thrust. They flew higher and higher, out over the bay, to the south toward Plymouth. What a thrill!

"Do you know why birds fly south?" Lloyd cackled.

"Because it's too far to walk!"

"That's an old one," said Mariah. It wasn't every day she got to ride high in the sky on the back of a heron, and something very strange was happening to the world below. All of the houses along the bay and the church steeples inland that poked up through the trees seemed to be dissolving before her eyes. As they came even with the Myles Standish Monument, it slowly melted away into the air, granite twinkling as the particles disappeared. What was happening?

A turkey vulture, wings spread wide, sailed high above like a kite in the breeze. "Did you hear the one about the vulture that got on a plane with two dead raccoons, one under each wing?" Mariah leaned forward to hear better. "The flight attendant stopped him and said 'I'm sorry, but you're only allowed one carrion.' Get it? C-A-R-R-I-O-N?" Mariah couldn't help laughing as Lloyd clacked his beak. Lloyd himself was much funnier than his jokes. "No baggage on this flight," he quipped.

How wonderful it was to see the world around her from this high vantage! But what was even more interesting was how the brick smokestack of the old cordage factory and the four tall antennae of the radio station, whose red lights blinked day and night, just fell away, sparkling into nothingness.

As they passed over Bug Light it shimmered and dissolved into the churning water between Saquish and Long Beach.

Big tour boats, yachts, and fishing vessels all vanished into thin air, along with the wharfs and fried clam shacks. Each thing shimmered and sparkled like fairy dust as it disappeared, as though the energy it had taken to create it was being put back into the universe.

"I think I get it," she whispered. "Life and death is like that. The energy comes and goes. The universe has the energy all the time. Just like the nows in time."

"Like compost," said Lloyd, startling her. "And speaking of death," he said, as they were lifted up on an air current. "Old sailors never die, they just keel over."

"Argh," said Mariah, thinking she'd have to tell her dad that one.

Down below there were no telephone poles, no pavement or parking meters along the waterfront, no jetty reaching out into the bay, no Mayflower in the harbor, no Plymouth Rock with its fancy portico. Just a few simple skiffs and canoes rested on a sandy spot in the eelgrass.

He turned a wide circle over the marsh where some

snowy egrets were wading in the shallows. "And how about that heron uncle that couldn't attend my old man's funeral," Lloyd waited a beat. "He sent his egrets!"

Mariah groaned while Lloyd descended.

When they touched down on the marsh she jumped off, stumbled and righted herself. "Enjoy your trip." cracked Lloyd, as he glanced over his shoulder and took off across the marsh, leaving her there shaking her head.

Mariah smoothed her skirt. Wait a minute – she had been wearing her party dress, the dark pink one with pockets. What was going on? Her skin felt itchy. She looked down to find herself wearing a dress of rough blue wool covered with a dingy linen apron, and on her feet were cobbled shoes. She reached into her apron pocket and was relieved to find her spearhead. The marsh grass was damp and golden. Mariah thought of Nelson when she saw hundreds of horseshoe crab shells scattered about the seaweed along the shore.

She had been to Plymouth a few times before, but it looked very different now. Where the Town Brook flowed out there was a small harbor, a pond that flowed out into the bay instead of the soggy park she'd walked in with her family earlier in the fall. She looked up at the sweeping hill that rose from the shore. Instead of all the hubbub of the modern tourist attraction, all she saw were a few small dwellings with thatched roofs.

Little dried up gardens fenced in with rough wooden rails stood along the dirt paths, and further off, a sweeping meadow of spent goldenrod, the same flowers that had made Travis sneeze.

She couldn't believe her eyes; it was more beautiful than she ever could have imagined, even on this gray November day. There was a newness about everything, and she breathed deeply so as to take it all in, to understand where she stood in time, in this now.

She stepped through the marsh, past the boats, and started walking cautiously up a steep path towards the settlement. A couple of native men walked towards her. She smiled up at them, but they took no notice of her. They dragged their canoe across the marsh, and paddled off. The canoe was a *mishoon,* the name she remembered from a field trip her class had taken to the Wampanoag village museum. It was made from one big, long hollowed-out log.

As she reached the settlement, she was surprised to find so many people. There must have been nearly a hundred Wampanoags, the native people, dressed in deerskin and feathers. They were beautiful people with dark hair, straight noses and high cheekbones. These must be the People of the First Light that the fox and Nelson had talked about. Some were playing drums and rattles and wooden flutes, making a kind of music Mariah had never heard before.

There were many tables outside between the dwellings in the center of the settlement. Rabbits, pheasants, geese, and ducks were laid out on one long table, while at another, busy Englishwomen and young boys skinned, plucked and prepared the game for roasting. On other tables there was even more food in carved wooden bowls and black iron pots. Mariah watched as an English boy placed two bowls, one of berries and one of chestnuts, on the table. The bowls were made from big horseshoe crab shells, upside down, just like the one Mariah carried her shells home in on the day she met Nelson.

A girl, dressed in clothes just like Mariah's, sat on a log next to a pot of steaming water, plucking a Canada goose and dropping the feathers into a basket. Mariah came up close to the girl and said hello, but the girl didn't see or hear her. The trip on Lloyd's back must have made her invisible.

Some natives came up the hill with strings of plump codfish. Englishwomen scurried about, turning meats on spits and stirring pots of bubbling stews. The cool air of the settlement was thick with the smoke of cooking fires and roasting meats.

A hush grew over the lively crowd as group of teenagers dressed in deerskin stumbled into the settlement with a deer they had killed. Its hooves were bound to a carrying pole that was bowed by the animal's dead weight. Its big brown eyes were open, but there was no expression on its face, only emptiness. They lowered it to the ground just as another small party came in behind them. More and more natives came, and with them, five deer in all. The words *Massasoit* drifted from many lips to Mariah's ears.

One native man stood out among the rest. Mariah thought he was the most handsome man she had ever seen.

An Englishwoman went inside a dwelling and came out with a man she introduced as Governor Bradford. The Governor spoke loudly as he greeted his special guest, Massasoit, the chief of the Wampanoag tribe. Mariah kept hearing the word *sachem*, the native word for king. Massasoit presented the five deer to the Englishman in a small ceremony. Englishmen came forward to pay their respects and inspect the deer and compliment the hunters.

The musicians began to play again. As they moved in rhythm through the crowd, even the beads on their deerskin dresses made music. A young English boy started jumping around and dancing, but his mother scolded him and made him stop, warning him about dancing and the devil. The Wampanoag smiled among themselves, whispering the words, *adamacho matta*, and somehow Mariah knew they were saying that the dancing boy certainly was not the devil. People seemed to be talking all at the same time in many languages. Even the English talk sounded foreign to Mariah's modern American ears.

Men were showing each other their firearms, sighting down barrels and inspecting little bags of ammunition. A group of natives squatted in a circle smoking a long pipe and talking with some of the Englishmen, while others stood about trading hunting stories.

All at once the men and boys headed off together, up and over the crest of the hill and out of sight. The musicians followed, leaving the others behind to prepare the food.

Mariah jumped as explosions of gunfire filled the air. She made her way carefully up the path toward the puffs of smoke rising up over the top of the hill. The banging and booming was so loud, she had to cover her ears. When she got to the crest of the hill she saw men and boys, mostly natives, loading firearms, and shooting them up in the air. Some of them seemed to be having contests on how quickly they could load and shoot, ramming long rods down the barrels of these funny-looking guns, and firing at a ragged piece of deer hide hanging from the branch of an old tree.

A boy about her age was looking at her. He was dressed in deerskin. Mariah had gotten used to being invisible, so this was perplexing. She walked towards the boy, astonished at how much he looked like Kip. He smiled at her, just like Kip did on the school bus and in Mrs. Tarbox's classroom. It *was* Kip!

"Can you hear me?" she asked Kip.

He nodded. "Ha ha," he said, not like a laugh. He was saying yes in his language, the language of Massachusett.

"How is it that you are here?"

Kip shrugged.

A small group of English colonists walked by talking about heathens and God's wrath and punishment falling upon them.

"Do they see you?" she asked.

"Ha ha," he said.

"Well, they can't see me! Look!" Mariah did a little jig right in front of a bunch of men as they came up the path.

Kip laughed. One of the native men gave him a funny look, and said, "Great Blue, what has gotten into you? Don't you know these Englishmen think celebration is a solemn occasion?" His friends laughed at his joke.   Mariah watched him with great interest. He was dressed in fancy deerskin and carried a staff.

The one beside him, the handsome chief, nodded with a knowing smile, "Yes, they prepare for feasting with fear in their eyes. They fear the Great Provider. *"Ascom quom pauputchim!"* Thanks be given to God, Mariah heard him say with a smile.

Another chortled, "The Wrathful Provider, hmmm… Where ever did they get the idea that Great Spirit is so angry? Must be some tale they heard across the big water."

The stately Massasoit, waved his hand at the settlement. "Here, we bring them five deer to feast on, and all they can talk and pray about is how their Great Spirit will punish them!" They laughed and laughed as if this was hilarious.   "Can't they see that joy is the Creator's greatest gift?"

"Another broke in, "How can they think Spirit is angry when they are met with such bounty?"

"Speaking of bounty," the man turned to Kip, "son, go upstream and fetch the little fish trap at headwater. Bring the bait down to share with these people."

Kip nodded, turned to Mariah and gestured for her to follow.

Up over the rise they ran, past the edge of the settlement, and down the other side of the hill along the little harbor and up to where the brook flowed in. A *mishoon* was resting on the bank.   There, in the bottom of the boat was an old empty horseshoe crab shell sitting in a couple of inches of water. Kip grabbed it and scraped it against the bottom, scooping up the water and tossing it overboard. "Those horseshoe crabs sure are useful," she said.

Kip shook the water out and placed it on his head like a helmet. He pointed up into the oak trees. "Beware of falling nuts," he laughed and knocked on the hard shell before dropping it back into the bottom of the boat.

Mariah looked at the swirling water around her. "Is there a native name for this brook?" she asked.

"Patuxet," Kip replied as he held the boat steady for her to get in. "This place is Patuxet." He pushed off, jumped in, and began paddling up the sluggish stream.

She opened her palm to show him the spearhead.

"*Cassaquot,*" he said. "A weapon of peace."

Nelson had said that, too. "What do you mean, a weapon of peace? Aren't weapons for fighting?"

"No," said he, "*Cassaquot* is a weapon of peace, a giver of life. We throw the spear to get food to eat and share. *Cassaquot* brings peace to our families, clothes to keep us warm, and comfort to our hungry bellies."

"Hmm, that makes sense," she said, looking at Kip and wondering how he could be there. "Kip, do you know me?"

"Of course," he said.

"Are you here from the future, too?"

"I am here now," he answered.

"Now," she repeated, "in this now." She looked at the wilderness around her and was very glad to be in that now, to know it firsthand.

Kip paddled upstream, jumping out here and there to pull the boat over small rapids, until they reached a pond, the headwater that his father had mentioned. Mariah knew the pond as the Billington Sea. There was a funny story about how it had been named. A boy who had sailed from England with his family climbed a tall tree and saw this shining water in the distance. He claimed to have discovered this new sea, like some great explorer.

The sea was really just a pond. So, as a joke, they named it the Billington Sea, and the name stuck. "What do you call this water, Kip? Oops, I mean Great

Blue."

"Patuxet," said Great Blue again, "this place is Patuxet."

"I know it as the Billington Sea, named after a pilgrim boy."

"Pilgrim?"

"An English boy, a colonist named Billington."

"Oh, Francis the troublemaker," Kip shook his dark ponytail knowingly. "He ran away from his settlement and came to our camp. He tried to shoot us, but his gun didn't work. We painted him up like a chief, and he thought that was dandy. He's always causing mischief of one kind or another. Now he comes often to our camp. I think he wants to be Wampanoag," he laughed.

"They call you Great Blue?"

"At my birth, my parents saw the spirit of the Great Heron emerge, so they honored that spirit by giving me its name."

"Well, you certainly are patient and quiet, so I guess the name fits," she said, and then thought again about how Lloyd the comedian didn't quite fit that description.

Kip beached the *mishoon* and jumped onto shore. Mariah slipped her shoes off and followed him along the mossy edge. He pulled on a finely spun cord, bringing up a trap made of vines. Many small silvery fish flipped and flopped and danced and jumped about inside like lively silver pieces.

"And look here," Great Blue exclaimed, "I am the catcher of small fish even in this human body!" With a delighted cackle that sounded just like Lloyd, he reached into the trap as if it were a pirate's treasure chest and threw a generous handful of fish back into the water. "I do not take all. Grandfathers say, 'We do not inherit the earth from our ancestors, we borrow it from our children.' So I try to remember to give some back for those who come after me."

Mariah remembered what the fox had said about the People of the First Light knowing only of sharing, not owning. The silvery fish plopped and splashed into the water. Kip laughed some more, very pleased with himself.

Mariah watched them glint and glimmer as they danced around her toes, and when she looked up again Kip was gone. Only his laughter remained in the cool autumn air.

Before she had a moment to wonder what had happened, she saw the great blue heron standing next to her, his long neck craned over the shallow water. She stood quiet and still, afraid she might scare him away or disturb the fish at her feet. In a blink the heron stabbed his beak into the water, came up with a wiggling fish, flipped it into the air and swallowed it in one gulp. He looked at her and winked. Mariah laughed, and her laughter carried her all the way back to the little beach at the end of the lane.

The itchy dress was gone, but the spearhead was still there, solid stone in her pocket. The echo of her laughter had followed her home, and whom did she see there at her feet, half buried in the mud? Nelson, of course, and Mariah could hear his deep laughter, too.

She looked at herself in the shimmering tidal pool. "Okay," she said, "I've traveled by wormhole and slipstream, but this was different. What happened? I was flown somewhere else!"

"No, not somewhere else," he corrected, "some*when* else!"

"But how?"

"Will o' the wisp," he whispered with a low chuckle. "When laughter gets mixed with the gas of the marsh, funny things can happen."

"Lloyd, Aaron's son, came and flew me across the bay to Plymouth!"

"On *wispwing*," said Nelson. "On the wings of laughter."

"Hey, how did you get here?" Nelson was not in his usual place. "It's a long way from the big beach for a slow-moving creature like you."

"I was blown over by that brisk northeast wind at the new moon, and helped along by the highest tide of the year. It was astronomically high!"

Mariah remembered how high the tide had been.

So high it had flooded the street near the Bluefish River and come into the parking lot at Snug Harbor. She remembered the northeast wind pushing the big waves over the seawall at the end of the lane. She imagined the moon and sun lining up, and all that gravity pulling on the water and lifting Nelson up.

"Astronomically high," she agreed, impatient to tell of her adventure. "Well, I just blew in from Plymouth on *wispwing*! Oh, Nelson! I went to the feast. There were so many natives, maybe a hundred, and really not so many pilgrims at all! And hardly any women."

She was talking so fast, trying to tell her story as if it were a dream she might forget at any moment. "There were no fat turkeys, but I saw lots of other things to eat. The Indians, I mean the Wampanoag, brought five deer. The natives didn't understand why the pilgrims were afraid of God. The men all showed off their guns. I saw my friend, Kip. He was Wampanoag. Great Blue! We took a canoe, a *mishoon*, up the Town Brook to the Billington Sea. But they didn't have those names yet; it was all called Patuxet. And Kip was the spirit of the heron, and when he laughed about the wiggling fish, he disappeared and Lloyd, I think it was Lloyd, replaced him, and I laughed when he ate a fish, and ended up back where I started!" She finally stopped to catch her breath.

It was getting dark and cold. Mariah looked down at Nelson in the mud. "So, now that you've been blown over here, how do you get back?"

"It is no coincidence that the northeast winds of late autumn have brought me this way. It's a good spot to hunker down for the winter. I'll burrow under the mud out by the channel where the water won't freeze. In the spring the warm west wind will send me back to the summer beach."

Mariah shivered. "No more mud for me today. I'm freezing here without a jacket." She didn't want to leave because she never knew if she would see Nelson again. But it was getting colder and darker by the minute.

"Okay," she said, "You go bury yourself in the mud out there, and hopefully we'll meet again in the spring." She remembered her encounter with Travis.

"I guess it's time for me to go home and face the music."

"Hmm," said Nelson, "Face music? Not listen?"

"Yes, face the music, not listen."

Today was Thanksgiving. Uncle Joe and Travis came. Travis is going to be living here until the end of school. I can't stand him. He's so mean. I wish he'd go away. His parents got a divorce, and Aunt Cheryl is in a mental institution. Uncle Joe said something about her

being an alcoholic and being in recovery. She's really nice and I love her and I hope she gets better.

I went down to the little beach and Travis followed me and was throwing rocks at me, and I threw mud at him. ☺ *Boy, was he mad. But I didn't get in trouble. I was laughing really hard and Lloyd the son of Aaron the great blue heron came by and he flew me over to Plymouth! To the real Thanksgiving! It was amazing. They were making all kinds of food like deer and ducks and stuff, but no turkey. I was invisible except to Kip, who was called Great Blue since he had the spirit of the heron. The Indians were really cool. They all wore deerskin and feathers and beads.*

I saw Massasoit and Governor Bradford. They weren't anything like what I'd imagined from history class. I didn't eat the food but I went upstream with Great Blue to get some fish from a trap, and before I knew what happened, I was back at the little beach. Nelson was there. He said I'd traveled by wispwing! Laughing and low tide gas made the will o' the wisp magic. It was really cool to fly over and watch things disappear.

Aaron died but Lloyd wasn't sad or anything. Everything that ever lives dies, and that's a fact, so why be sad? Animals are pretty smart, and

Lloyd was very silly like a bad comedian. Nelson said he will spend the winter in the mud near the channel. I sure hope I find him next spring. I wish Travis would disappear.

Chapter VII

Travis

One cold evening Mariah's father made good on his promise about the fireplace. They collected kindling and brought an armload of logs from the woodpile up to her room. Her dad knelt at the hearth and asked her, "What's the first thing you do when you are going to make a fire?"

Mariah thought about getting the wood and paper and matches, but she knew he was asking for a different answer. She shrugged as her dad stuck his head into the fireplace and pointed up into the chimney. She looked up and saw the soot-covered damper and its notched handle. "You open the damper," said her dad. "The first thing you do, every time, is open the damper, because if you don't you'll wish you had!" He opened the damper, and then closed it again. "Now you do it."

Mariah pushed the heavy handle up until it caught on the last notch with a satisfying clang. She had opened an avenue of air, and could feel the draft move past her on its way up the chimney. Her fingers were black with soot.

Her dad showed her each step of fire-making, and then had her do it herself. First twisting the newspaper, adding the kindling, and then the logs on top, and finally, after checking the flue again to make absolutely sure it was open, he had her strike a match and hold it to a twisted piece of newspaper. He waved it slowly back and forth in the fireplace, watching the smoke rise up the chimney.

"Establish the draft," he said as he handed the torch to Mariah and guided her hand to light the fire. Mesmerized, they watched the fire take hold. He gave her a few more safety tips before he left her alone in her room with her own fireplace.

The smell of the burning wood made her remember Thanksgiving and her magical trip on wispwing. It all seemed like a dream now. She filled her kettle, and hung it on the hook, all the while fancying herself a pioneer about to do her homework by the firelight.

Mariah didn't like having to share anything with Travis, especially her life. His unpleasant underarm odor hung around in the air even after he had left the room. His bedroom was right next to hers, and the pink roses on the wall between them quivered with the smashing, shooting, beeping and explosions of his video games. Mariah thought it was unfair that Travis had a television in his room. She wasn't even allowed to watch TV on school nights let alone have one in her room. He hogged the computer playing his games when she was trying to use it for homework. She had to admit, though, he didn't have a fireplace, and all of the electronics in his room did keep him occupied in there. But school was another story.

The bus ride was only the beginning. Travis spent his bus rides switching between the backseat where he would make faces and gestures at the cars behind the bus and the seat behind Mariah. It was as though he always knew when she wanted to be left alone. He would sit behind her and pull her hair and tease her in rhymes. *Mariah, Mariah, pants on fire.* He looked around, and if no one was paying attention, sang louder. *Miller, Miller, looks like a gorilla!* Mariah shook her head and muttered under her breath, "Your last name is Miller, too, you dumbbell."

When Kip took his usual seat beside her, Travis yelled, "WOO WOO!," and sang, *Mariah and Kippy, sittin' on the bus, kissin' and huggin' and makin' a fuss. First comes love, then comes marriage, and then comes little Kippy in the baby carriage.*

Mariah and Kip talked quietly about how Travis' taunts weren't very creative or original. If they succeeded in ignoring him, he resorted to other things to rile them, such as leaning over the back of their seat, putting his face between them, and making loud, juicy smooching noises. One time he even brought a couple of snowballs on the bus and dropped them down their backs when they were unsuspecting. Mariah didn't mind so much. It was just snow. She remembered the mud.

Travis had been kept back in kindergarten, and then again that year, so instead of being in eighth grade, he was in sixth. As luck would have it, he was assigned to Room 6B, and Mrs. Tarbox had put his desk right next to Mariah's. In addition to his smelly B.O., he was always looking over at her work and copying from her paper. Mrs. Tarbox never seemed to notice.

It was the day of an important math test. The test counted for a big part of the winter term grade. Math was Mariah's worst subject. No matter how hard she tried to be interested in it, it just held no excitement for her. During math class Mariah's eyes glazed over and her mind wandered to places far away from the classroom. She had drawn some of her best pictures during math.

Mrs. Tarbox was handing out the tests while everyone put away their books and papers and sharpened their pencils. It was a steely cold gray day outside, so dark that the lights in the classroom shone inside on the windows as if it were nighttime, and Mariah saw her own reflection when she looked out.

She had stayed up late and gone over and over the problems from her worksheets and textbook to prepare for the test. She felt fairly confident that she would get a good grade. Travis, on the other hand, had not studied at all. When she asked him at breakfast, he had said, "I don't need to study. I'm good at math, and I already had that last year."

Travis drummed his pencil on his desk.

Mrs. Tarbox called the class to order. "You will have exactly forty minutes to complete the test," she said, looking up at the big round clock. "Begin."

There were forty problems. Mariah looked at the clock: forty problems and forty minutes to do them.

About halfway through the test she noticed that Travis was copying from her work. She gave him an angry look, and draped her arm over her paper.

With six minutes remaining Mariah felt sure that she could count on getting at least a B+. Only three problems left, and she would be finished. Travis pushed her elbow aside so he could read some of her answers. Mariah whispered, "Stop it!" and hovered closer over her work. Mrs. Tarbox looked up and growled.

As Mariah finished problem thirty-nine, an idea popped into her mind. It was time to teach Travis another lesson. It might cost two-and-a-half points off her score, but it would be worth it. She read the last question: *An object weighing 5 pounds on Earth will weigh 2 pounds on Mercury. A blue whale weighs 110 tons. What would the whale weigh on Mercury?*

Mariah thought that was easy enough; it is two-fifths. She divided 110 by 5 to get 22, and then multiplied that by 2 to get the answer: 44 tons. She looked up at the clock to find she still had a few minutes left to put her plan into action. Just yesterday Mariah had learned that one pound equals .4536, nearly half of a kilogram. She multiplied the whale's 44 tons by 2000 to get 88000 pounds, and then multiplied that by .4536 to get 39916.8 kilograms for her answer.

Math seemed a little easier when revenge on Travis was involved. The answer was correct, but she used kilograms instead of tons. Maybe, she thought hopefully, Mrs. Tarbox might even give her extra credit, and Travis would have to stop cheating.

With a minute left on the clock, Mariah sat back from her paper and watched out of the corner of her eye as Travis copied that last answer.

"Eyes on your own paper, Miss Miller," warned Mrs. Tarbox.

Mariah closed her eyes and put her pencil down just as the bell rang.

The next day Mrs. Tarbox kept Mariah in during free period. "Do you know why you are here?" she asked from behind her desk.

Mariah stood on the other side of the desk. Her face was red hot and her heart was beating so hard she could hardly speak. "I think so," she said, thinking that finally Mrs. Tarbox would move Travis' desk away from hers and punish him for cheating.

The teacher reached into her desk, opened a folder and brought out the two tests. Mrs. Tarbox tapped the last answer on Mariah's paper with her red pen. "What's this?" she asked as she circled the answer with a bold flourish. "I do not tolerate cheating in this classroom! There is no way you both could have gotten this answer. And I saw YOU looking at your neighbor's work!"

Mariah was stunned, almost too stunned to speak. It was Travis who cheated. She began to explain. "I put that answer to trick…"

Mrs. Tarbox stopped her short. "There is no excuse for this type of behavior!"

"But…"

"Let this be your first and only warning, Miss Miller. Any future offense will result in suspension."

"But I did the extra work," Mariah pleaded. "I multiplied the pounds by .4536 to get the answer."

Mrs. Tarbox was not listening. She was busy uncapping her pen again. She marked Mariah's math test with a big red F and then circled it saying, "It takes two to cheat like this!"

Mariah did not know what that meant. Nothing seemed to make sense. All she did know was that, no matter how hard she tried to please Mrs. Tarbox, her efforts always backfired. She understood math well enough to know that the F on her test would make a D on her report card. She had never gotten a D or even a C in her life. It seemed like her whole world was falling apart.

Mariah hadn't mentioned it to her parents, but she knew the report card would arrive any day now.

Even though it was still winter, she could sense that spring was on its way. Chickadees and nuthatches sang new songs. Downy woodpeckers rattled away high up in the trees, and grackles squeaked like rusty hinges up in the high branches of the bare maple tree. One day it thawed, the next day it froze. The days were getting longer, and the earth was slowly warming so that the ground was both hard and muddy.

When Mariah got home from school, she was surprised to see her dad home from work so early on a weekday. She came in through the mudroom to find him sitting at the kitchen table with a pile of mail. Her mom was standing at the counter wiping her hands with a dishtowel. Travis had walked to a friend's house after school, so the house was pleasantly devoid of him and his B.O.. She headed toward the stairs with her backpack.

"Mariah," her dad called out in a foreboding tone. "Please come here."

She dropped her book bag at the bottom of the stairs and returned to the kitchen. Looking back and forth between her mother and father, she noticed that they both wore the same expression of raised eyebrows and pursed lips. Her report card must have arrived.

Mariah got a terrible sinking feeling as her dad pulled the card from its envelope, unfolded it, and started to read down the line. "English, A-; Social Studies, B+; Science, A; Math, D. What's this about?" Her father tapped on the card and pointed to the chair for her to sit.

She saw the A in Physical Education and the A in Art, wishing they mattered as much as math.

Mrs. Miller stood with her arms folded across her chest, looking over Mr. Miller's shoulder, waiting for Mariah's explanation.

"I'm sorry," Mariah said. "Travis was cheating off my paper, so I tricked him with a special answer, and Mrs. Tarbox thought I cheated and gave me an F." Mariah fought the tears welling up. "But I didn't cheat, Travis did."

Her parents went on to talk about how cheating is a two-edged sword that hurts everyone involved. They were sympathetic towards Travis because of his broken home and allergies and bad situation, which made Mariah feel even worse. "You, of all people," her dad said, "could have a little compassion. Put yourself in his shoes."

"Impossible," said Mariah, thinking of his big stinky sneakers.

Mr. Miller raised his voice. "You can care about a toad on the side of the road, but you can't have a little sympathy for your own cousin?"

"But, Dad," she whined. "He's so mean! He's always been mean. He's never been nice. And he cheats. And he's always trying to hurt me. He's always teasing me and getting me in trouble."

Mariah's dad laughed. "Your uncle Joe always used to get me in trouble."

"He did?"

"Yes, he did. And even though he was the troublemaker, he always came up smelling like a rose."

"Well, Travis stinks!" huffed Mariah.

Mr. and Mrs. Miller looked at each other sideways. They had to agree. Travis did have offensive body odor.

"Next time I go shopping, I'll get him some deodorant," her mother promised with a smile, as if underarm deodorant would resolve everything.

Her dad gave her a big hug. "You'll recover. Sometimes you learn more than just reading and math at school."

Mariah sighed, and went to the mudroom to get her jacket and boots. Travis was a fact of her life, just like Mrs. Tarbox. There was no escape, so she might as well just accept things the way they were, and concentrate on bringing up her math grade.

She headed down to the end of the lane. The air was cold, the tide was nearly high, and the afternoon sun glistened like liquid silver on the bay. A small flock of mallard ducks took off from the marsh, wings whistling, making low, magical music that ended with a unified swoosh as they glided onto the water.

A larger flock of eider ducks paddled out by the channel. They moved in unison and made a droning sound as if the whole flock were one smooth mechanical thing. The whirring and clicking reminded Mariah of the sound of a music box between the notes—a little machine inside the big machine of the universe.

She walked along the edge of the marsh, jumping over the ditches. Each time she landed, a splash of cold salty water dampened her pant legs just above her boots. She got lost in the rhythm of walking and watching the marsh for ditches and holes to jump over. She walked and watched and jumped, staying as close to the edge of the marsh as she could without sliding off into the frigid bay.

Mariah sensed someone watching her, following her. She stopped and looked at the water, but there was nothing there. She turned around half expecting to find Travis behind her, but he wasn't there. She looked up at the houses and lawns along the shoreline. All was still and quiet, so she continued on.

She bent down and picked up the hard, mahogany-brown shell of an old horseshoe crab. "Phew," she said when she saw that this crab had all of its tail. Looking out across the cold water at the red channel marker,

Mariah wondered where in all that cold, gushy mud Nelson might be sleeping. She picked up the shell to take home and add to her collection in the mudroom.

Mariah just felt it in her bones that she was being watched, but she did not feel threatened or afraid. Instinctively, she felt for her spearhead in her pocket, relieved to find its familiar shape beneath her mitten. She decided she would keep walking along the marsh towards Shipyard as far as she could go.

It was then that she saw her companion. It was moving along in the water, silently keeping abreast of her as she walked and jumped along the marsh. It looked like a cute, earless dog with big eyes and funny, broad whiskers that reminded her of a cartoon character. But it wasn't a dog. Its coat was the soft gray color of a mouse but deep and plush with the sheen of velvet. It was so close she could reach out and touch it. But she didn't; she just kept walking and jumping. When she stopped, the seal stopped. When she walked faster, the seal swam faster, watching her every move with its big round eyes.

She came to a ditch that was too wide to jump over, so she turned around to head back home. The seal vanished under the water.

The rising tide had started to come over the marsh, widening the pools and running through the eelgrass, making it difficult to jump over the ditches without slipping and splashing. She came to a ditch that had flooded over, and just as she was about to leap across, the seal popped up right in front of her.

"Hello, my friend," she said gently. He looked a lot like the creature she had helped in the streamtime, only he was smaller, and gray instead of brown.

"Hello, my friend," the seal mimicked.

Mariah tried not to act surprised. She was very casual, as if she talked to seals every day. Her voice was soft and smooth. She didn't want to scare him away.

"Do I know you?"

"Do I know you?" he repeated.

"What's your name?" she asked.

"What's your name?" said the seal.

"I asked you first," she said.

"I asked you first," he said.

Mariah couldn't believe it. Here she was, talking to a real live seal, and he was teasing her just like Travis did! His big dark eyes sparkled with mischief, but she was willing to put up with teasing from a seal, just because, and only because, it was a seal.

"Will you be my friend?"

"Will you be my friend?"

"Yes!" she said excitedly.

"Yes!" said the seal.

Now that was settled, maybe he would cooperate. "Aren't you cold?" she asked.

"Aren't you cold?" said the seal.

This was exasperating. "Warm and dry, actually," said Mariah, even though it wasn't true. Her pants were soaked up past her knees, and her feet were so cold her toes had gone numb. If that seal said he was warm and dry, she might as well end the conversation now.

"I'm warm and fat," said the seal.

"I guess you are," agreed Mariah.

"I guess you ain't!" The seal submerged for a moment and popped back up. Mariah jumped over the ditch, landing with a big, slippery splash on the other side. She thought she had better head home before the tide swallowed up the marsh completely. The seal traveled with her in the rising water alongside the marsh.

They stopped for a moment. She looked at him, trying to understand how such a beautiful creature could be so annoying.

He gave her a quizzical look, and then he burped a huge, obnoxious belch. "Ahhhh," he said, satisfied.

Mariah recoiled at the rancid fishy smell of his breath. But more so, she was offended by his rudeness. "Excuse me?" Mariah said just as her mother would have.

The seal replied, "What did ya do?" as if Mariah were excusing herself.

Mariah clicked her tongue and shook her head. "You are so soft and beautiful. How can you be so fresh?"

"Fresh?" He laughed. "I is very fresh!" He burped again.

"Yes, fresh and smelly."

"You smelt?" he asked.

"Yes, I smelled your fishy breath."

"You smelt smelt," he said.

"I smelled," she said.

"No, you smelt Smelt!"

"Smelt? Oh, the little fish?"

"Yesiree, the smelt I ate and then you smelt!"

"Fine," she said, ignoring his play on words. "What kind of a seal are you?"

"What kind of a human is you?"

"*Are* you," corrected Mariah.

"Are you," copied the seal.

Mariah thought about this. She hoped she was a good human being, but this was more scientific. She asked again, "What kind of seal are you?"

"What name does you humans call me?"

"*Do* you humans call me," said Mariah.

"You calling me a human?" The seal was insulted and ready to pick a fight.

"No, no," said Mariah, hoping to smooth things over, "I asked you what kind of seal you are."

"What kind of a seal you are," he repeated.

"No no, what kind of a seal are you?"

"Here's a hint," he wisecracked, "Look around. Where is I?"

"Where *am* I," she said.

"You don't know where you is? You is on the marsh, you numbskull," he yelped. "I asked you, where is I?"

She tried to think of the seal species she had heard of. Hooded seal, gray seal, well, he was gray but that wasn't the hint..."Harbor seal?"

"Yessiree, my sister! And this is a mighty fine harbor, indeed!"

"Why did you just call me your sister?"

"Because we is all brothers and sisters in this world."

"We *are* all brothers and sisters," Mariah corrected.

"That's right," he agreed with a nod. "We is all brothers and sisters."

"My friend Nelson said that, too," Mariah said as she decided it just wasn't worth the effort to correct his grammar.

"My friend Nelson said that, too," the seal mimicked.

Mariah tried to think of something to say that would make the seal seem silly if he repeated it. "My name is Mariah. What's yours?"

"Sivart," he said.

Hmmm," said Mariah. "I've never heard that name before. How do you spell it?"

"Seals ain't supposed to know how to spell"

"Could you at least give it a try?"

The seal hesitated, and then began, "T – R – A – V..."

"Hey, wait a minute," she said. "That's Travis! Sivart is Travis spelled backwards! You're trying to trick me."

"You're trying to trick me," repeated Sivart.

"I have a fat cousin named Travis who is always trying to trick me."

"I'm fat," said the seal, "like your cousin. Is he a harbor seal, too?"

"No, he's a human, but you two have a lot in common." And she wasn't just thinking about the fat, either.

It was nearly dark as Mariah and Sivart reached the place where the marsh met the little beach. Mariah stood for a moment thinking how strange and bewildering this encounter had been. "It was very nice to meet you," she said.

"It was very nice to meet you," Sivart mimicked. "My regards to your fat brother Travis."

"He is *not* my brother," she declared, hardly hiding her irritation.

"Is I your brother?"

"You mean, *am* I your brother."

"You is a boy? I thought you was a girl."

Mariah laughed.

"Either way," he continued, "Like I asked you before: Is I your brother?"

Well," Mariah said thoughtfully, "Since we are all brothers and sisters in this world, I guess you are my brother."

Sivart gave a gleeful yip, and said, "Then, fat Travis is your brother, too!"

The seal dove under the dark water. Mariah wiggled her toes in her boots as she watched and waited to see if he would resurface. Just as she turned to go, she thought she saw his head pop up way out by the red channel marker.

I got a D on my report card. It really isn't fair. Travis is a cheater. It should be a B. I asked mom to call Mrs. Tarbox and get Travis's desk moved away from mine. She and Dad said that school is full of all kinds of lessons, and learning to get along with all kinds of people is one of them.

I met a seal today. He was very annoying. He teased and teased me just like Travis, and when I asked him his name he said it was SIVART. Then I asked him to spell it, and he spelled TRAVIS. Then he tricked me into saying Travis was my brother, which he is NOT.

Chapter VIII
Poetry

Big fat snowflakes fell straight down past Mariah's window and onto the porch roof below. It was the first day of March, and many of the flakes melted as soon as they hit the shingles. A large brown rabbit loped across the backyard leaving a trail of dark tracks in the murky snow. "Rabbit, rabbit," whispered Mariah, hoping the March Hare might bring her double luck.

She grabbed a piece of black construction paper from her desk, opened the window, and held the paper out flat until a perfectly plump snowflake landed on it. She brought it in, slammed the window shut, and ran down the stairs as fast as she could to show it to her mom before it melted. "Quick, look!" she said, surprised to see her dad at the kitchen table. He usually had left for work by that time. The snowflake melted before their eyes, leaving its wet, symmetrical signature on the paper.

Her dad smiled weakly. Something was wrong. His face was swollen and pale, and dark circles ringed his eyes. "Are you okay, dad?"

"I'm fine," he said rubbing his back, "just a touch of

the flu or something."

Mariah's mom turned from the sink. She wore a frown on her face.

"You missed my flake, mom. But look, you can see the shape." Her mom looked exhausted as she nodded at the black paper Mariah held out to her. Travis was shoveling cereal into his mouth. "Lemme see," he said, spewing milk down his chin. Mariah tossed the paper onto the table in front of him. He wiped his mouth with the back of his hand and a few splatters of milk fell on the black paper. "Big deal," he said.

Her mother had turned back to the sink. "Hurry up and get ready for school, you don't want to miss the bus."

All through the day in the classroom and during lunch and gym Mariah couldn't shake the image of her father's face. There was a dark, empty feeling lying deep in her chest. She felt like she had to remind herself to breathe to fill it up. It was harder than usual to keep her mind on the schoolwork, and Mrs. Tarbox kept calling on her. The class was studying poetry, and the teacher had given them twenty minutes to write a poem. Mariah had been thinking about her dad, and then her encounter with Sivart the harbor seal, how he had said the same thing Nelson had about everyone being brothers and sisters. She wanted to write a poem about that, but she wasn't sure how to begin. She had been making little animal doodles on the paper, and when she realized she only had a few minutes left, she wrote frantically, right off the top of her head

Of course, Old Tarbox called on her first. Ever since Uncle Joe called her that, the name had stuck. She had learned from the report card that her first name was Mildred, and that seemed fitting. But just plain Old Tarbox was even better. Mariah looked around her. Most of the kids were still hunched down writing. Travis was rocking back in his chair and looking at the ceiling.

Taking a deep breath and blowing it out, she held up her paper and read. "My poem is called 'Relations'."

> This is my petition.
> Please be quiet and listen
> To the message of others
> Our sisters and brothers
> Hear the songs of the sea
> And the birds in the tree
> They are all our relations
> Just like you and me.

The class was quiet. Beside her, Travis was slumped in his chair, and drumming his fingers on his desk. He reminded her of Sivart the seal, and how he had fooled her with his word tricks.

"That was lovely, Mariah," Mrs. Tarbox said, "except it should be, 'you and I' as you and I are relations. I am. We are."

Mariah cringed at the thought. Relations with Old Tarbox? Sivart popped back into her mind just like he had popped up in the water. She just couldn't win.

As quickly as Mrs. Tarbox had corrected her, Mariah shot back, "Well then, And the birds in the sky – Just as you and I."

Old Tarbox nodded, and something near a smile came across her face.

The teacher called on Travis next. Mariah rolled her eyes as Travis unslumped himself and stood up beside his desk. He didn't even reach down for his paper; he just stood looking straight ahead. "I wrote a haiku," he said.

Old Tarbox nodded approvingly since they hadn't talked about haiku in the class yet, but it was on the list of types of poetry they were going to learn. Travis cleared his wheezy throat and patted his chest dramatically, getting a laugh from some of the kids.

Dust on the floor floats
A cloud on linoleum
Escaped the push broom

"Oh my," said Mrs. Tarbox. "Very good, Travis."

How cheap, thought Mariah as she looked down at the dust ball on the floor while Old Tarbox waxed poetic about the haiku form and the sparseness and truth of Travis's observation. She thanked Travis for introducing haiku to the class.

When Mariah and Travis got home from school that afternoon there was a note on the kitchen table. She read her mom's hastily scribbled words out loud to Travis who was deep in the refrigerator looking for a snack. Her mom had taken her dad to the hospital in Boston for some tests. They were supposed to be back by dinnertime.

"Ya," said Travis slugging back some orange juice straight out of the carton, "he didn't look too hot this morning." He burped. Mariah was worried.

"Ya know," he confided. "My mom's in the loony bin."

"She's not in the loony bin," Mariah said shaking her head. "She's in a psychiatric hospital."

"Same thing, different words."

"Well, she's getting better."

Travis's cheeks were puffed out from a big mouthful of leftover cake. He just shrugged.

Mrs. Miller arrived home alone. She had left Mr. Miller at the hospital overnight so they could stabilize him. "Kidney failure," she said when Mariah asked what was wrong. "They're not sure what caused it, but that's what he's got." Mrs. Miller's eyes were red from crying, but she put on a smile for Mariah.

"Is he going to die?"

"Everyone's going to die, Mariah, sooner or later. They're taking good care of him at the hospital, and he should be home tomorrow. She held Mariah close, almost too tightly. *Everyone's going to die sooner or later.* Those words sounded a lot like what Lloyd had said about his father. She wasn't ready to have her dad be the late Mike Miller. "Do you ever pray?" she asked her mom.

Her mom thought for a moment, and said, "If thinking good thoughts and wishing the best for everyone is praying, well then, I guess I do. I'll be thinking lots of good thoughts for Daddy, that's for sure!"

Mrs. Miller put a handful of papers and pamphlets the doctor had given her on the kitchen counter. Mariah saw the scary headlines: Living with Dialysis, Kidney Disease, Donor Information, Your Dialysis Diet.

"Now, go do your homework. He'll be home tomorrow. He'll be fine," her mom said.

Mariah asked her mom if she could light her fire upstairs. It was a chilly night. But more than that, she just wanted to be by the warming light of the fire.

"Okay," said her mom, "just a small one, and make sure to use the screen." Along with the kettle for Christmas, her parents had given her a fireplace screen to keep the hot embers from jumping out into her room. "Keeps embers out, but lets Santa in," her dad had joked, holding up the screen like a TV pitchman.

Mariah had already laid the fire. All it needed was a match. Up on the mantel, along with the matches and a neat row of baby horseshoe crab shells, she found her spearhead just where she had left it nestled on a piece of cotton in a small wooden box. She felt the stone in her hand; it was more precious to her than a jewel. She never knew when its magic might arise.

Kneeling at the hearth, she reached up and pushed the heavy damper handle up until it sighed with a clink sending bits of soot down onto her hand. She peeked up to make sure it rested on the handle's lowest tooth. Even though night had fallen, a special kind of light filtered down through the chimney. It was the cool light of a big round moon shining in the eastern sky. A flock of Canada geese honked above, echoing the promise of spring.

Mariah struck the match to a piece of newspaper. The kindling crackled and snapped as the fire took hold, sending fairies of warm light dancing about her room, and casting a golden blush on the wallpaper roses. She had her books there, feeling like Abraham Lincoln doing her homework by the firelight, but she couldn't stop worrying for her father.

Was he going to die? Could she be like Lloyd and know that it's okay that everybody dies, even when it was her own father? What would her mother do? A cold, dark shadow crept over her, leaving nothing but a big empty feeling, a loneliness she had never known before. Despite the crackling fire, she shivered like a small, frightened animal. She saw her dad's smiling face, heard his laugh, and longed for him to pick her up and squeeze her tight. She imagined him in a hospital hooked up to a machine.

"Oh, Daddy, please get better," she whispered as she worried the spearhead around in her fingers. Through her tears the hot colors of the fire blurred together like a river of heat going up the chimney. When she realized she was crying out loud, she put her hand over her mouth so Travis wouldn't hear her, and cried even harder. "Please don't die, Daddy," she pleaded.

She thought about praying. Was praying like wishing? Wishing seemed too simple, and praying seemed like begging or making a deal. Maybe her mom was right, good thoughts are the best prayers.

"We make our own heaven or hell right here and now," her mom had said when Mariah asked about it.

Mariah realized that her mom seemed more like the People of the First Light. "Just be fair. Follow the Golden Rule. Do unto others as you would like done unto you."

She remembered how Great Blue had tossed some fish back, and how The People of the First Light spoke of the Great Creator being kind and generous. Maybe, she decided, the best kind of prayer was to concentrate on good things, to trust that everything will be okay. She put her spearhead down on the hearth, folded her hands and formed her prayer carefully, whispering in the firelight, "I am grateful for this warm fire and my wonderful dad who teaches me so much. May all good things come to my father." She started to say amen, but changed her mind. "So be it," she said as she dried her eyes.

The spearhead rested on the warming bricks of the hearth, its facets reflecting the yellow firelight. She spun it a few times, like the spinner on a Twister game, wondering where it would point.

Now it kept spinning all of its own, spinning and spinning, rising upwards, helicopter-style. Mariah reached out to catch it before it rose into the flames, and when she did, she too started spinning and spinning, spiraling up the chimney as if she were a vaporous wisp of smoke. In fact, she was! So much for the homework for now, she thought, for this *now*.

Up, up she went, right up the chimney and high into the sky. "Honk honk," she said. She beat her wings faster and faster until she found herself aligned with the flock, taking up her place as the wingtip of the chevron, the V-shaped formation of geese in the sky. What a thrill to feel the wind passing her as she flapped and flapped her wings. She did not know where she was going and she didn't care.

"So this is how it feels to be carefree," she said as she effortlessly aligned her sight with the forward goose's tail feathers. And on they went over the water and under the moon that shone its glistening path below.

I must be in a parallel now, she was thinking as she flew along.

The lead goose fell back to the position behind Mariah. "Honk," said Mariah, "Why did you come back here?"

"All tuckered out, my dear. Move away from the flock and see what happens."

When Mariah veered off from her position behind the goose ahead of her she felt such drag and wind resistance she swerved right back into formation. Wow!" she honked. Some of the other geese honked too, "Go, go, go! Good job!" They honked their encouragement to the lead goose.

"The goose in front of you creates an uplift, just as you are doing for me. We get seventy percent better range when we fly this way. If we flew on our own, we'd be very tired birds. We take turns being point goose."

Amazing, thought Mariah, how these geese know how to cooperate.

"Honk, honk," said the goose in front of her as they headed inland flying low over the tops of tall pines. She followed as the flock descended one by one onto a shimmering moonlit pool deep in the woods. The white birch trees and dark pines both reflected and made moon shadows on the shiny water, reflections of reflections and shadows of shadows.

They paddled about little islands of tufted grasses. New green shoots were working their way up through last year's dead brown growth. Mariah saw herself reflected in the water, her graceful neck with its brilliant white marking and her shiny black bill. The geese gaggled and gossiped about each other as they plunged their necks deep into the pool, pulling up weeds to eat.

"Oh, take a gander at that gander," whistled one.

"And he's a good egg, too!"

"Take your eyes off him, gals. He's taken!" hooted another.

"Don't get your feathers ruffled, dear."

While all of this honking and gaggling and chatting and eating went on no one noticed the gray coyote moving carefully from behind a boulder toward the pool. Her legs were bent and her belly nearly scraped the leafy ground as she licked her chops, and slinked toward the edge.

A fat goose paddled over to Mariah. "Why so glum," she asked.

"I'm worried about my dad."

"Why worry? What will be will be."

"But he has kidney failure." With that most of the geese perked up and paid attention.

"Kidney failure in a goose?" they exclaimed. "Liver pâté, maybe, but not kidney failure."

"No, he's a human."

"Go figure," said a tall gander. "They don't eat right, and they use too many chemicals and make bad trash." He grabbed a slimy potato chip wrapper with his beak and tossed it off to the side.

"How old is he?"

"Forty-one," said Mariah.

"Forty-one," exclaimed a goose. "That's a ripe old age. Geese don't last that long!"

"Especially at hunting season," whistled another.

"He's not a goose," Mariah reminded them.

"Well, he's already outlived our kind by a decade," said a gander with pondweed hanging from his beak. "We're lucky if we make it to thirty!"

"I think he's what's called middle aged by their standards," said a goose.

"Twice that of a mallard," another honked.

"Thrice that of a toad," said another, as if she were getting points in a game show.

"Quadruple a grouse!" one piped in quickly, "and

ten times a mouse!"

"Alright, alright. I get it," squawked Mariah.

The yellow eyes of the coyote shown in the moonlight, but the geese were making such a racket nobody noticed. Her bushy tail gave a quick wag just before she struck. In a flash, she leapt at the closest goose, her sharp teeth clamped onto the slender black neck like a trap. Mariah heard the snapping of bones.

All at once the geese squawked and hooted, "GET OUT, GET OUT, SCOOT SCOOT SCOOT," as they took off en masse up through the tall trees. As she flapped her wings to join the flock, Mariah turned back to see the coyote drag the flailing goose off into the woods. Two geese stayed behind, but when they saw that it was hopeless, they took off, too.

"Honk, honk," said the goose ahead of her. "That was a close one."

Mariah reported that the coyote had dragged the little goose into the woods.

"Everybody's got to eat," honked the goose.

Travis was knocking on her bedroom door telling her it was time for dinner. Mariah looked at the spearhead in her hand. What was that all about? She wished Nelson were there to explain to her what had happened. When she had gone to the ice age, he said she had gone by wormhole. When she had swum through the streamtime, it had been a slipstream of her tears, and when she flew on Lloyd's back backward in nows to the first Thanksgiving, she had gone on wispwing. Earth, Water, Air, and now Fire had taken her to other nows.

She wracked her brain. Fire, smoke, heat, draft, updraft—*updraft*—that's how she had gone right up the chimney. The updraft had uplifted her. Her worries had carried her up to a place where, at first she thought she was carefree, but then she found out that it was the goose in front of her and her own cooperation that had made her flying easy.

She stirred the fire with the poker, put the screen carefully in front, and went down for dinner.

Dad has kidney failure. He's in the hospital. Mom brought all these pamphlets home about it. They have stupid pictures on them that try to look friendly but just make me more scared. He needs dialysis (however you spell it) where a machine cleans his blood. I can't imagine if he was gone forever. I hope he doesn't die – yet. Really I hope he never dies. He is the best dad. I am so worried I don't know what to do. I

know everything has to die but I sure would like it if my dad could live more.

I ♡ him soooo much.

I went up my chimney in the smoke and was a goose. They are very smart. They cooperate by taking turns being in front so they can fly further. A coyote ate one of the geese. The other geese didn't seem sad. They said everybody has to eat. I had chicken for dinner so I'm no different than a coyote, I guess.

I hope Dad will be okay.

Chapter IX
Obstacles

Mariah sat in the classroom hardly listening to Old Tarbox talk about Sir Isaac Newton and gravity and his idea of an ordered universe. She was wondering if her dad was going to be okay when she heard Mrs. Tarbox say, "Albert Einstein's Special Theory of Relativity."

Mrs. Tarbox said that Sir Isaac Newton thought time, space, and mass (the amount of matter in stuff) were constant and unchanging, but Albert Einstein didn't think so, so he used the astronomer Galileo's earlier theory of relativity to create his own Special Theory that was based on the idea that different points of view make things relative. She said, "Einstein found that it was impossible for time, space, and mass to remain the same from different points of view."

She had Mariah's full attention now. All of her travels to other nows flashed before her eyes. So, she thought, maybe it's just my point of view that takes me to those other nows?

Mrs. Tarbox stood at the front of the room. "For example," she said looking at Mariah in her seat near the back of the class, "You are a distance away from me, so you look small to me and I look small to you. That's because my size is relative to where you are. From here, I'm the same size I always am, but to you I look smaller."

Mariah was thinking Old Tarbox still looked pretty big, but she wasn't going to argue. She looked over at Travis who was actually paying attention. Travis had grown taller and thinned out in the past few months. He had played basketball all winter, and had signed up for baseball. His skin was better, too, and he had stopped being so mean. He still teased her a lot, but now it was more in fun.

The teacher went on talking about the speed of light and how Einstein used his imagination about traveling incredibly fast to discover relativity. She paced back and forth behind her desk, and said, "He also came to the conclusion that energy has mass, and that mass is increased by speed, which is how he cooked up his famous $E=mc^2$ equation." She wrote it on the board, along with E=energy; m=mass, c=speed of light, and said, "He realized that mass is simply potential energy that's standing still!"

Mariah remembered how things dissolved when she traveled back in time on wispwing with Lloyd.

"So," said Mrs. Tarbox, "Relativity explains that atoms are really just tight groupings of energy. It also accounts for different points of view, and takes into consideration that what you think is real could be completely different when viewed from another perspective."

Mariah was so excited she raised her hand before she even knew what she was going to say. Her shyness had given way to her curiosity. Mrs. Tarbox lifted her chin and raised her brows. "Mariah?"

"What about time? What did Einstein think about time?"

"Einstein said time, in absolute terms, does not exist, that it's relative to the position and speed of the observer."

Mariah didn't even think to raise her hand again. "Time is relative," she blurted out.

Mrs. Tarbox nodded invitingly. "Yes, and please explain what you mean by that."

Mariah felt the cold cloak of shyness press down on her, making her heart beat too hard. All of a sudden she didn't want to talk; she wasn't sure what to say. She thought for a moment about how she had gone into other nows while still being in the one she was in; how sometimes nows can change really fast like cards in the hands of a magician. Then in other nows, like this one, where she felt shy and nervous, time seemed to stand still. How was she going to explain that?

She took a deep breath and began with a stammer, "Y, y, you know when..."

Old Tarbox interrupted her before she could continue. "No, we don't know, Mariah; why don't you tell us?" She was smiling kindly at Mariah, but from Mariah's point of view it looked like a vicious sneer.

Mariah, all flustered, started again, "You know..."

Mrs. Tarbox jumped in again, embarrassing her. "No, we don't know; please tell us."

"It's like..."

"As if," Mrs. Tarbox corrected. "It is 'as if.' When you use the word 'like' in this class, you will be using the verb that means 'to be fond of' or 'want to have'; or the adjective meaning similar."

Mrs. Tarbox kept catching her in these word traps. Mariah was in too deep to sit down and give up. She had to be very careful. Slowly and cautiously, she crafted her words. "Every moment is a now in the present. But maybe time can be like a deck of cards; stacked together and all existing at the same time, past and future, like, oops, such as remembering something and worrying about something that could happen all at the same time as just being."

Mariah winced, not knowing if she was making any

sense at all. Mrs. Tarbox encouraged her with an interested nod.

"Sometimes, bad memories or worries about the future get stuck in a moment and make time seem thick and slow. Now, and before, and after, all get stuck together. Then a moment seems bigger, longer…" She was about to use the word 'like' again, as in 'like right now' but she caught herself just in time.

Just then, at that very moment, Mariah realized that if she could just change her point of view and leave the past behind, just the past few moments, she would be free of the horrible feeling clinging to her right now!

Her heart stopped pounding. A new power rose up, and she looked Old Tarbox straight in the eye. "An example is right now. Right now I could be in the past remembering how embarrassed I was a minute ago, and my moment would be crowded and heavy, and time would slow down. But if I change my point of view, not just my speed and position, then this moment is a brand new now!"

Mrs. Tarbox smiled at her. "A brand new now," she said. "Einstein thought more about time in the sense of physics, but Miss Miller, you have just demonstrated how the concept of time has baffled and excited philosophers and scientists alike since the beginning of time! Whenever that was."

The kids who were paying attention laughed all at once. Mariah sat down in her chair. Some of the kids were looking at her like she was nuts. Or were they? How could she know their point of view? She looked over at Kip, the quietest kid in the class. He craned his neck forward like a heron.

"Anyone else?" the teacher asked.

For the first time in that whole school year, Kip raised his hand. Very quietly, he asked, "What about time travel? What did Einstein think about time travel?"

Mrs. Tarbox was shocked and pleased. The only time Kip ever spoke in class was when she called on him.

"According to Einstein, time travel is theoretically possible." She started drawing pictures on the board and talking about how the speed of light is constant in space, and if you were traveling in a spaceship at nearly the speed of light, time would seem to pass for you just as usual.

Mariah was impressed with Old Tarbox's funny drawings. "So, you are up in space and you write your name. That takes just a few seconds, right?"

The kids were nodding. Mrs. Tarbox went on.

"But, if someone, say your twin brother, were to observe you from down on earth, if he could, it would seem that you were writing an essay, taking hours, even days!

"Now, say you turned your spaceship around and returned to earth. Traveling so fast, you had been gone for two years, and you had aged only two years.

But, thirty years had passed on earth, and now your twin brother was much older than you! That is how Einstein's theory accounts for the possibility of time travel into the future."

Mariah's hand popped into the air of its own accord. "What about going back in time?"

Mrs. Tarbox sighed. "In general relativity theory, you might, by way of a *wormhole*..."

Mariah's ears got hot as Mrs. Tarbox went on. "But quantum mechanics makes that very improbable. As the great physicist Stephen Hawking said, 'Nature may have made the past safe for historians.'"

Mariah had never been more confused in her life.

She knew what she knew whether science knew it or not.

Mrs. Tarbox could see her bewilderment. "Buddhists consider time as nothing more than an illusion." She looked up at the big clock on the wall just as the bell rang. "And now it's time for gym."

When Mariah got back from school her dad was home from the hospital, resting on his chair. He gave her a hug and groaned. "Found out what this backache is all about," he said. He patted the hassock in front of him for her to sit down. "It's my kidneys, or what's left of them."

"Are you going to be okay?" she asked.

"It's a very serious thing, " he said. "You need your kidneys to clean your blood, and mine aren't doing their job."

Mariah held her breath, trying not to cry.

"But don't worry, honey. I'll be getting dialysis three times a week up at the hospital. The dialysis cleans my blood just like kidneys do. And there's a diet to follow. I can say goodbye to those fat juicy steaks." He rubbed his back. "There's no cure for it, but they put me on a donor list."

"A donor list?" said Mariah. "What do you mean?"

Mr. Miller explained that the only way for him to live a normal life was to get a donor kidney from someone whose blood type and some other factors matched his. Many people need replacement kidneys, so the hospital put him on a waiting list.

"You can have one of my kidneys, dad," she said hopefully, just as her mother came into the living room and set a cup of tea beside his chair.

"That's a very generous offer, dear," said her mom. "They did mention that a family member might be able to be a donor. Not kids, though."

Mrs. Miller left the room, and came back a few minutes later holding two little cards in her hand. "When you were born the hospital gave us each a card with our blood type on it." She handed the cards to Mariah. "I'm B-positive and so are you. Daddy is type O. And it's not just blood type; there are other factors that have to match."

"What about Uncle Joe? Maybe he has type O," said Mariah hopefully.

Mr. Miller put his face in his hands. "I could never ask someone to donate a kidney to me. It's a big operation, and there are lots of risks. I could never expect someone to do that."

"The donor list is pretty gruesome, too, " said Mrs. Miller. "Waiting for somebody healthy to die so they can harvest the organs..."

Just then the backdoor slammed. "I'm home," called Travis.

I learned a lot of science stuff today. I couldn't believe it when Mrs. Tarbox said Albert Einstein thought you could travel back in time through a WORMHOLE. But then she said newer science guys don't think it's really possible. But I know it is.

Dad is really sick and he has to get kidney dialysis 3 times a week to clean his blood. He needs to find somebody or some BODY, I mean DEAD body with type O blood and a bunch of other stuff to match. Maybe Uncle Joe can give him a kidney. I looked it up on the internet and they don't act like it's such a big deal to get one from a living person. Seems like a big deal to me.

Chapter X

Stepping Stones

The warm afternoon air of springtime felt bittersweet to Mariah when she opened her bedroom window. Dappled sun waved among the bright green leaves of the maple trees surrounding the yard. The air was alive with the sounds of busy birds about their springtime business: the creaking of grackles, the tweeting of chickadees, the chirping of robins, and the cawing of a crow. Mariah wondered what they were saying.

Her dad was spending more and more time at the hospital, and although he was receiving kidney dialysis three times a week, he still looked pale and sick, and his back hurt all the time. Uncle Joe had come to visit for a week, sharing the guestroom with Travis. Over the weekend she could hear the two of them playing video games, whooping and laughing and crashing and beeping on the other side of the wallpaper roses.

One morning Uncle Joe drove Mariah's dad up to the hospital. While Mr. Miller was having his dialysis, Uncle Joe had his blood tested to see if he could donate a kidney to his brother.

For three days they waited on pins and needles for

the news from the lab. Once the results were in, Uncle Joe sat everyone down in the kitchen and sadly reported that he did have the same blood type, but he still wasn't a match because he didn't have the right antigens.

"What are antigens?" Travis asked.

"They're something in your white blood cells that help fight infections. If the antigens don't match, then Uncle Mike's white blood cells would fight the kidney cells, like they were an infection." said Uncle Joe.

"The attack of the alien antigens!" whooped Travis, making video game noises.

Everybody gave a nervous laugh. Travis made a small bow. "Comic relief," he said. The whole family sat around the kitchen table wondering what to do next.

It was the time of year when, in the past, the Millers were planning a move, but not this year. As her dad had promised, they were staying put. But now, he was so sick he had to stay near Boston and the hospital.

At least school wasn't such a drag. Mrs. Tarbox spent more time doing fun and interesting things with the class, taking them outside to sit on the grass in the sunshine for book discussions, and walking through the conservation land behind the school for science, drawing pictures and keeping a nature journal.

Mariah had started to wonder how someone who had been so mean in the beginning actually seemed really nice lately. Remembering Einstein, she figured it might have been her point of view. Maybe Mrs. Tarbox hadn't changed at all; maybe it was Mariah herself who had changed. Time may not exist, she thought, but change sure does.

That day, Mrs. Tarbox led the class in the election of class superlatives. There were categories for most studious, most likely to succeed, class clown, most talkative, friendliest, most athletic, most popular, and so on. The kids wrote a name in the space next to each category on the ballot, and Mrs. Tarbox tallied up the scores. Mariah had filled in her ballot knowing quite well who would be voted the best dressed and most popular girl: Karen, the blonde junior cheerleader she had bumped into on her first day, who ignored Mariah most of the time. Karen's boyfriend Jonathan, the sailor with the perpetual tan, would be voted the most handsome, best dressed, and popular boy.

Mrs. Tarbox began reading the winners' names and handing out little certificates. Kip was voted the quietest. As predicted Jonathan and Karen were most popular and best dressed. When she heard her name called for most artistic, she blushed as she went up to collect her certificate. Then, Mrs. Tarbox read the results for the prettiest. She said that Karen had taken the popular vote, "but I am exercising my executive power here, and I vote for Mariah Miller because she has the most beautiful eyes."

Mariah's beautiful eyes widened in disbelief. No

one but her dad had ever said anything like that to her ever in her life, and this was Old Tarbox. The teacher went on to say something about having seen how hundreds of kids have turned out, and she felt herself the best judge. She held out two certificates. Too stunned to be shy or embarrassed, Mariah went up and got her certificate. On her way back to her desk, Kip winked at her.

Travis was voted class clown, even though Mariah had voted for another kid. Since he was absent that day, Mariah brought his certificate home for him.

Travis wasn't sick or anything, but since Uncle Joe would be leaving soon, they had taken a "personal day," just the two of them. Mariah was thinking that maybe the next time she didn't feel like going to school, she'd ask her mom if she could take a personal day. Fat chance, she thought as she leaned over her windowsill listening to the birds, and worrying the spearhead around in her fingers.

Just as she was about to turn back into the room, a big black crow landed on the sill, tipping his shiny head back and forth, looking at her with one beady eye and then the other. "Shape-shifter," he cawed.

"What?" said Mariah.

"Shape-shifter," said the crow. "My, my, how you change, you little trickster."

Mariah was indignant. If there was one thing she wasn't, it was a trickster, whatever that was.

"I beg your pardon?" she huffed.

He cocked his head from side to side. "Look at you, all tall and lovely." That was the second time in one day that someone had said something nice about her appearance. She couldn't help but smile. "What's a shape-shifter?"

"Caw, caw," he sang his song. "We are the keepers of sacred law. Man's law is flaw, flawed. We bend those laws of Newton and Einstein. We change time, any ol' time. We shift our form; there is no norm... because we are the shape-shifters," he went into a big crescendo, "We are the shape-shifters... of the world!"

Mariah laughed.

Crow peered up at her with one shiny eye, and opening his thick black beak, said, "Pssst. You want to know a secret?"

"Oh, yes," said Mariah.

"Don't tell anybody or we'll lose our mystique, but

anybody can be one."

"One what?"

"A shape-shifter, for crying out loud! What do you think I've been singing about? Why do you think I paid you this caw?"

"You mean, paid me this *call*?"

"No, I mean, paid you this *caw*!"

"What's a shape-shifter?"

"You are! You're a master of illusion. First you're all shy-like; then you're all smart-like; then you're a beauty queen...if that ain't shape-shifting, I don't know what is."

"A beauty queen?" Mariah batted her eyelashes, "Maybe that's an illusion."

"Looked in the mirror lately?"

"Well, no, not really."

"Go do it now, I'll wait. Come back and tell me what you see."

Mariah went over to her bureau and looked in the mirror. It took a moment for her eyes to adjust to the darkness inside the room. She studied her reflection. No longer was she the timid girl who had been pushed into room 6B last September; she had grown tall, and her eyes shone with confidence, just as Nelson had said: clear as the sky and true blue.

The crow stood on the windowsill as she stepped back from the mirror. "So, tell me, shape-shifter, what did you see?"

"I saw myself," said Mariah. "I'm growing up."

Crow gave a wolfish catcall. "Quite the babe!"

Mariah's cheeks flushed. She looked down at the spearhead in her hand.

The crow hopped along the sill to get a better look. "What's that you've got there?"

She held her hand out so the crow could inspect the spearhead, first with one eye and then the other.

"Nice," he said. "Crow loves nice shiny things like that." He hopped a little closer. "The People of the First Light made it. Weapon of peace. Crow likes it." He darted towards her hand to snatch the stone with his beak just as Mariah snapped her fist shut around it.

"Ouch," she said.

"Give it to me. I want it."

"No!"

"Caw, caw, come on," he whined. "Plueeeeeease?"

"I'm sorry but this is my treasure. I can't give it to you."

"Haven't you learned anything?" he said in exasperation. Crow slowly turned his head and looked at her with the other eye. He said, "Ah hum," cleared his throat, and spoke in a different voice, deep and pure. *"The love of possessions is a weakness to overcome. Its appeal is to the material part, and if allowed its way, it will disturb the spiritual balance. You must learn the beauty of generosity. You must give what you prize most, that you may taste the happiness of giving. If you are inclined to cling to your little possessions, you will be told legends about contempt and disgrace falling upon the ungenerous and mean..."*

"I'm not mean," argued Mariah. Crow wasn't listening. He was pacing back and forth, a shining black silhouette on the white-painted windowsill.

"The People in their simplicity give away all that they have—to relatives, to guests..." he shot her a glance, *"but above all to the poor and aged, from whom they can hope for no return."* Crow gave his black head a meaningful nod. "Those are the words of the great medicine man, Ohiyesa, a.k.a. Charles Alexander Eastman, M.D. I took some liberty with the quotation, but you get the point, right?" He waited for a moment.

"I get the point, right?" he said, eyeing the spearhead.

"Wait just a sec," said Mariah, remembering what she had heard about crows loving shiny things. She ran to her bureau and opened her little jewelry box. A ballerina popped up and started going around and around to a tinkling *Dance of the Sugarplum Fairies*. Crow was humming along as he hopped daintily about on the windowsill. Mariah chose the shiniest, gaudiest thing in the box, a bracelet she had made with large metallic beads. She clapped the lid down on the ballerina, ran back to the window and dropped the beads onto the sill.

"Here," she said. "I made this. Would you like it?"

The beads were blinding in the sunlight, casting

dazzling reds and purples and blues onto the windowsill. Crow looked at it first with one eye, and then the other.

"Hmm, nice trinket," he said. "Now are you going to try and sell me the Brooklyn Bridge?"

"No, I just thought you'd like this better."

"Okay, but you can't have Manhattan."

"Huh?"

"And I happen to know that there are bigger plans for the point."

Mariah looked down at the spearhead wondering what the crow meant. Crow rolled the beads around on the sill, admiring their brilliance.

"Will you accept my gift?"

"Accepted," said the crow as he took the bracelet in his beak, and flew off up to the top of the tallest tree.

Mariah watched him, perched up there, swaying on the highest branch, the bracelet glinting in the sun. Another crow landed on the same branch. Crow leaned forward and gave the beads to the other bird before they flew off together.

I can't believe it. I got this certificate for the PRETTIEST!!!! The other day Mrs. Tarbox asked me if my ears had been ringing, and you know what? They were the night before. She said she and some other teachers were talking about me. When somebody talks about you, I guess your ears are supposed to ring. She said don't worry, they were saying very nice things about me. I wonder what they were saying. Mrs. Tarbox seems like a different person OR maybe it's me who is different.

The Crow called me a shape-shifter. He said I was a babe! Well, I'm not, but it was nice of him to say that. Crows love shiny things. He tried to steal my spearhead but I gave him my shiniest bracelet instead. He went for it, but he gave me a lecture about possessions. This is the third time an animal has mentioned the People of the First Light. They didn't own things. They shared and gave away.

Dad isn't doing so well. I hope they find a kidney donor soon.

Chapter XI
Brothers & Sisters

Travis was missing a lot of school having personal days with Uncle Joe, but they usually got back in time for Travis' baseball practice. They had been going to Boston a lot, Museum of Science, Fanuel Hall, the Aquarium, they said. Mariah wished she had been able to go to the Aquarium. That day they had driven to Connecticut. When they came back to the house they whispered quietly as if they were part of some kind of a conspiracy.

"Hey, I saw my mom today," said Travis as he rummaged through the refrigerator looking for a snack. "We went to court in New Haven."

"Oh, how is she?" asked Mariah. Aunt Cheryl had always been her favorite. She sent cards to her in the hospital, and got a note back every now and then.

Travis emerged with a carrot, holding it up like a prize. "She's out of the looney bin and seems good. She's on medicine that helps her. They were being quite, what's the word they use for divorces? Amicable, they were friendly—amicable," he said, swinging the carrot around like a saber.

"Anyway, she met some guy in the program, and

they're moving to California. In court Mom gave Dad full custody of me. Dad says for now your parents are my guardians. Mom says I can fly out to California for visits. I always wanted to go to the coast." His bottom lip trembled around his forced smile. Mariah turned and opened the fridge so as not to embarrass him.

The next afternoon the whole family went to Travis' baseball game. Mariah stood and waited while Uncle Joe helped her dad out of the car. He was thin and pale, and he had dark circles under his eyes. Uncle Joe held his elbow as they walked slowly from the parking lot to the bleachers.

They were late getting to the game. Travis was playing center field. "That's my boy," said Uncle Joe as Travis caught a high fly ball for the third out in that inning. The visitors were ahead five to four. The bases were loaded, and the home team had two outs when Travis stepped up to the plate.

"Go Trav, go!" yelled Uncle Joe, as Travis swung at a low ball for the first strike. He hit a foul ball on the next pitch, and everyone groaned.

Mariah found herself cheering Travis on, too. "Come on, Travis! You can do it!"

On the third pitch, Travis whacked the ball high and long, over the fence for a home run. He loped around the bases, bringing the score to eight to five. He looked handsome in his baseball uniform, and Mariah was proud of him. Uncle Joe, Mrs. Miller and

Mariah jumped up and down whistling and cheering with the rest of the hometown fans. Her dad stayed in his seat and clapped.

The last inning seemed to go on forever. By the time the visitors had two outs, the score was eight to seven with two men on base. The next batter, a big kid, bigger than Travis, looked ominous as he stood at the plate. He swung and missed, and then he swung and hit a high fly ball into left field. Travis stepped back until he was right under it, and caught it to end the game with a win.

"That's my boy!" yelled Uncle Joe. Mr. Miller stood

up and let out one of his shrill two-fingered whistles.

"Yay, Travis," screamed Mariah while all of his teammates clapped him on the back as they headed for the dugout.

Afterward they all went out for ice cream to celebrate. Mr. Miller just drank water.

Towards the end of Uncle Joe's visit, he announced at the dinner table that he was going to be staying a while longer. He winked at Travis who looked side to side at the family. "Can I tell, Dad?"

"Yep, Trav, this is your show."

Mariah couldn't figure out what the heck was going on. Travis looked at her, and then at her parents. "Dad and I have been going to the hospital. I had all the tests, even seen the shrink a bunch of times..." He nodded, making sure, even though they didn't know what he was talking about, that they got it. He looked at Mariah's dad and said, "Uncle Mike, I'm a match! And I have permission to give you my right kidney!"

Mr. Miller was shaking his head. "No, no," he said, "I won't allow it. You're too young. It's just too dangerous."

"Actually, Uncle Mike," he said, sounding like a doctor, "any surgery has risks. But Dad and I have been talking to the doctors, *and shrinks,* and it's really okay. I'm a perfect match! "

Mike Miller looked at his brother. "We can't do

this. It's irresponsible. He's just a kid."

"I'll be fifteen soon," said Travis. "I've had all the tests and am as healthy as a horse! That's what they said at the hospital, healthy as a horse, with the heart of an athlete!" Travis flexed his muscles. "And Mom said it's okay, too."

Uncle Joe had tears in his eyes. "Brother, if I were a match, you'd take my kidney in a heartbeat. Travis loves you very much and hounded me until I took him for the tests. We've talked to the counselors, passed the psychiatric workups, and they feel that he shows a level of maturity and altruism that is rarely seen, even in adults. You'd be helping him as much as he would be helping you. That's what they said."

"And now they have a new kind of surgery where they don't cut you open so much. What's it called, Dad?"

"Laparoscopy."

"Right, and I only stay in the hospital for a couple of days. And my recovery is pretty quick, just a few weeks. I'll hang around here and Mariah and Aunt Linda," he winked, "can wait on me hand and foot. Right?"

Mariah's mom nodded; tears were streaming down her face. Suddenly Mariah saw Travis from a completely different point of view. He was willing to undergo risky surgery to help her father. Tears poured from her eyes, too.

"All we need to do now is have some family

counseling, make sure everybody's on the same page, and then, when school's out you can schedule the surgery," said Uncle Joe.

"I can't do that," said Mr. Miller shaking his head, "it's just doesn't seem right. You're up for Babe Ruth league. It would ruin your season."

Travis looked like he might cry, too. "Uncle Mike, you're not getting any better, and I really want to do this. I can play baseball next year. You're like a dad to me, and I don't want to lose you."

Now everybody in the room was crying. Travis jumped up and brought a box of tissues in from the kitchen, and they all blew their noses.

I take back every bad thing I ever said about Travis. He really has changed. Maybe he's a shape-shifter too. He really is a good guy. Today he said he'd give Dad his right kidney. It makes me think about the crow and the People of the First Light. Giving a kidney is much bigger than just giving a prized possession like a bracelet or spearhead. It's giving part of your self! Dad says he doesn't want Travis to have the operation and only have one kidney for the rest of his life. He says it would be irresponsible because Travis is just a

kid. Travis has grown up a lot since he's been here. I never thought I'd be saying this but I really like Travis, and whether he gives Dad his kidney or not, he is my brother now. I guess that seal was right.

Chapter XII
Points of View

inally, the last day of school arrived. "So, what are your summer plans?" Mrs. Tarbox asked the class, pointing at each student to take a turn. Most of the kids talked about going to camp, sailing lessons or family trips, or just hanging around. Karen was going to cheerleading camp. Jonathan was going to Martha's Vineyard. Kip would be traveling to the Grand Canyon with his family. Mariah was volunteering at the Oceans Lab, the oceanographic laboratory up the street. She had been hanging around there asking a lot of questions and offering to help out, so they offered her the volunteer job.

When Travis stood up, he said, "I'm hoping to donate my right kidney to my uncle." The kids all laughed thinking he was joking since he was, after all, the official class clown.

"No, seriously," he said. "He's really sick and has kidney dialysis three times a week, and he needs a donor, and I'm a perfect match. But he hasn't completely agreed to it yet, so it's not a done deal. If I were a grownup, he'd probably be fine with it."

"That's quite a sacrifice to make," said Mrs. Tarbox.

"Whether it happens or not, Travis, I applaud you for your compassion and willingness to undergo such an ordeal for another human being." Mrs. Tarbox started clapping, and then everyone in the classroom clapped and cheered for Travis.

At the end of the day, Mrs. Tarbox bid her students farewell, and lots of luck in junior high. When the last bell rang and all of the students were saying goodbye and leaving, Mrs. Tarbox caught Mariah before she headed out the door.

"Mariah," she said as she opened her desk drawer. "I have something for you." She pulled out the picture that she'd confiscated in history class months ago, the unflattering portrait of Mrs. Tarbox. Mariah had forgotten all about it.

"Oh, Mrs. Tarbox," she said, "I am really sorry. That was so mean of me." She looked at the picture. She had made the teacher look like a mean old hag.

"No, Mariah. It wasn't mean. It was true. And I thank you for showing me how I looked to you. Your picture helped me immensely. You see, my husband had passed away after a long illness, and I was angry at the world, and I shouldn't have brought my bitterness into this classroom." She pulled another sheet from the drawer. "Here, this is for you."

Mariah took the sketch. It was a picture of a beautiful young woman with lovely eyes. It was a portrait of Mariah. "I don't really look like that," said Mariah. "She's too pretty and grown up."

"It's you," she said with a smile. "A perfect likeness, and it's my little gift to you. A gift for a gift."

"Thanks, " she said, slipping the pictures into her knapsack.

"Kids like you are the reason why I teach the sixth grade. In such a brief time, you grew from a shy, unconfident kid to a self-assured young woman. And, believe it or not, your artwork inspired me to take up my art again, too! So, we all learn things from each other." Mrs. Tarbox looked into her eyes with a kindness Mariah hadn't seen before.

"Remember when we were talking about Einstein and his relativity theory, and you said that somebody's reality depends on their point of view?" said Mariah. "It really is true. When I changed the way I looked at things, when I changed my point of view, the things I looked at changed!"

"Amen," said Mrs. Tarbox

Mariah and Kip shared a seat on the school bus for the last time. He was off to the Grand Canyon, and then to private school in the fall. "I'll miss you, Kip," said Mariah.

"Me, too," said Kip. "Don't forget to write." He handed her a feather. "I found this the other day. You can make a pen out of it."

"Hmm, it doesn't look like a gull feather. What kind is it?"

"Great blue heron, I think," said Kip with a wink as he hopped out of his seat and jumped off at his stop.

Mariah lugged her backpack up to her room and shoved it under her bed. Uncle Joe had gone back to Connecticut, and her mom had taken her dad up to the hospital for dialysis.

Just a week, and she'd be starting her volunteer job at the Lab. She would be working with the injured animals and keeping the tanks clean. They had sent a permission form for her mom to sign so she could travel with them to Woods Hole Oceanographic Institute on Cape Cod and to the Aquarium in Boston. She stood at her mantle arranging her horseshoe crab shells imagining what it was going to be like, when Travis knocked on her door. "Come on in, Trav," she said.

Travis stepped into her room in his baseball uniform and stocking feet. His socks were dirty from walking around without shoes on.

"I wish your dad would make up his mind," he said.

"It's kind of weird not knowing if I'm going to have the surgery or not."

Mariah picked up a little horseshoe crab by the telson and twirled it between her fingertips. "I know what you mean. It's like being in limbo, huh?"

"I don't know if I should try out for the Babe Ruth league or not."

Mariah reached up and brought down the small wooden box where she kept her spearhead. "I think you should try out anyway." She opened the box, and held it out to Travis. "You never know what might happen."

"Wow," he said. "An arrowhead! That is so cool. Where did you get it?"

"It's a spearhead. I found it on the bay side of the big beach." She took it from its cotton nest and handed it to Travis. He held it up to the light of the window, marveling at it.

"The Wampanoags, the People of the First Light, called it a Weapon of Peace because it gave them food and hides and stuff, so they wouldn't be hungry or cold."

"Wow," he said, "I get it, a weapon of peace. Cool!"

"I want you to have it," she said.

"Really?" Travis was shocked.

"Really. It's my favorite treasure, and I want you to have it."

"Why?"

"Because…" She thought about what Crow had said

about the People and the beauty of generosity, and she thought about how generous Travis was to want to give his kidney to her dad. "Just because."

"You sure?" Her turned it over and jabbed the point into his palm.

"Yep." She handed him the wooden box. "It's for good luck."

"Wow, thanks!" he said as he pointed the spearhead and pantomimed shooting an arrow. "No Indian giving, right?"

"No Indian giving," she promised holding up her hand like she was taking an oath.

Just then the phone rang in the hallway. Mariah ran to answer it. It was her mom calling from the hospital.

"Good news," she said, all excited. "There's a donor kidney that just arrived here on ice for your father. It's a perfect match, and as luck would have it, he was right here at the hospital when it arrived! Dad's going under the knife as soon as they're ready. I'll be staying over. You kids will be okay, right? I called Mrs. Smithson, and if you need anything, just knock on her door. Okay?"

"Okay." Mariah didn't know whether to be scared or excited or both.

"You can heat up that casserole in the fridge for dinner. Is Travis there?"

"Yep, he's right here."

"Put him on."

"Okay. Tell Dad that I'll be thinking good thoughts for him all day and night."

Mariah handed the phone to Travis and stood by while he listened. It seemed to take forever. Finally, he said goodbye and hung up. "What'd she say?"

"She told me about the kidney. And she told me that your dad wanted her to tell me that he was really grateful that I wanted to donate mine, but that he was really relieved he didn't have to take me up on the offer. I'm a little relieved, too," said Travis. "She also said, 'While I'm away, no monkey business from you, young man.'" He crouched into a chimpanzee stance, scratched his armpit, and hopped around on his dirty socks making jungle noises while Mariah giggled.

I've been so busy. Everything is topsy-turvy. Dad is getting a new kidney tomorrow. I'm scared. I hope it goes okay. I hope his body doesn't reject it. I read about it online, and sometimes that happens.

I gave Travis my spearhead. I wonder if it will make magic for him. I didn't tell him about the talking animals and traveling to other nows. Even if I won't be able to talk to Nelson ever again, it's worth it to give it to Travis. It's not like it's a kidney or anything.

Today was the last day of school. Mrs. Tarbox gave me back the nasty picture I made of her. She said she liked it because it made her know how she looked to me when she was bitter. She drew a really nice picture of me. I sure look good from her point of view. Uncle Joe was right about Mrs. Tarbox. She really is the best teacher I ever had. I never thought I'd say this but I'm going to miss her. I'm going to miss Kip too.

Even though we're not moving, things are changing so fast it's almost like moving anyway. Travis is going to stay here for the summer. Mom said he can stay forever if he wants to since we are his family. I hope he makes the Babe Ruth team now that he's not going to have the operation. I can't wait to start my volunteer job at the lab.

I wonder if I'll ever see Nelson again.

Mrs. Miller called in the morning and told the kids to keep busy and not worry, that she'd call after the surgery.

Travis and Mariah decided that the best way not to worry was to do a project, so they searched the garage for scrapers and sandpaper, and went to work on the *Kite.* Travis lifted the tarp that had covered her all winter while Mariah picked up a huge daddy longlegs in her cupped hands and blew it away onto the grass.

"Eek," screamed Travis as he danced around laughing.

"Little Miss Muffet," teased Mariah.

"Nice tuffet," said Travis as he patted the *Kite*. The boat was upside down, its hull like a big fat whale.

"I want to have her all ready to sail when dad gets out of the hospital," she said, as they each scraped and sanded furiously.

Travis found the paint and a couple of brushes in the mudroom. They worked hard all through the morning and into the afternoon. When the phone rang they both dropped their paintbrushes and dashed inside to get it.

Mariah let Travis pick it up. She put her ear close so she could hear. The operation had been a success, and now they'd just had to wait and hope his body would accept the new organ.

"Yes!" Mariah and Travis jumped up in the air and gave each other a high five with blue painted fingers.

"Wow," look at the time," said Travis. "I got to get to practice. Can I use your bike?"

"Sure," said Mariah.

Travis reached in his pocket and pulled out the spearhead. "This is really good luck, you know. I've been hitting real good."

Mariah was painting the last few strokes on the *Kite*'s bottom as Travis wheeled the bike out of the garage and jumped on. "Hope I don't look like a sissy riding a girl's bike," he said as he coasted out of the driveway in his baseball uniform.

"Nobody will notice," said Mariah. "Good luck!"

Mr. Miller was out of intensive care, and ready for visitors when Travis, Mariah and her mother drove up to Boston. As they navigated the hospital halls to find his room, they saw a young man in a bathrobe walking the corridor. He held onto an I.V. pole on wheels, pushing it along beside him. He smiled and said hello when they passed by.

As they peeked around the corner into his room, Mariah said, "Dad! You look great," though he looked pretty bad, but from her point of view, alive was great.

"Not quite great, but I'm getting there," said her dad.

"Uncle Mike, guess what?" said Travis. "I made the Babe Ruth team! I'll be playing my favorite position, center field. And I got a job mowing Mrs. Smithson's lawn. And don't worry, I'm doing your lawn, and taking out the trash, too."

Not to be outdone, Mariah said, "And we painted the *Kite*, and I start my volunteer job at the Oceans Lab tomorrow. "

"Right up your alley," said her Dad.

"Lucky Mariah gets to hang around with all of her animal friends in the muck and mud," said Travis, which made her wonder if he had made some animal friends himself since she had given him the spearhead.

"You thirsty, Uncle Mike? Want me to get you more water?" Travis picked up the empty pitcher from the hospital tray, and headed for the hallway. "I gotta check this place out."

"Don't get lost," said Mrs. Miller.

Mariah gave her dad the magazines she had brought for him. Mr. Miller showed them his scar, and the family chatted about this and that until Mr. Miller started to look tired. It was time to go.

"I wonder what's keeping Travis," Mrs. Miller said, just as he came into the room with the water.

As he placed the pitcher on the tray, he said, "Sorry, I got waylaid. I met this really cool guy in the hall. He's seventeen, and he gave his right kidney to his brother. He said it wasn't so bad. So, don't worry, Uncle Mike. If your body rejects the one you got from the donor, you can still have one of mine."

With hugs and kisses, they headed out of the room and back down the hallway. The guy in the bathrobe said, "Thanks, Travis!"

Mariah couldn't believe her eyes. He held the spearhead up, pointing it toward the ceiling. "With a little luck, I'll be going home tomorrow."

"How could you?" she whispered under her breath. "That was my best treasure I gave you." She elbowed Travis in the arm.

Travis ignored her. He raised his fists, giving the guy two thumbs up, and turning to Mariah, said, "You gave it to me for good luck; I gave it to him for good luck. Hope you don't mind."

"Oh, Travis," she said shaking her head. "I don't mind at all." But she did mind. Somewhere in the back of her brain, she had been thinking all along that maybe she might borrow it from Travis once in a while. And then, remembering Crow's lecture, she felt ashamed. A gift was a gift, period.

That crow was right. Travis gave the spearhead to this kid who gave his brother his kidney. When I saw how happy he was I remembered what the crow said about the People of the First Light. It made Travis happier to give it away than he was when I gave it to him! I kind of wish he'd kept it, but a gift is a gift, and once I gave it to Travis, it was his to do whatever he wanted with it. I wonder if that guy will go to other nows.

Dad looked pretty tired, but happy. I guess he'll have to be on a special diet for the rest of his life. He said he didn't care; it was just good to be alive.

Tomorrow I start my job. Even though they don't pay me, it's still a job. I am so excited.

Chapter XIII
Seal of Approval

The Oceans Lab was just up the street, so Mariah walked over in case Travis might need her bike to get to baseball practice. It was five minutes to nine when she marched up the steps onto the porch of the big yellow house where the offices were. She peered through the leaded glass window and took a deep breath before opening the door. A woman with reading glasses sat at the reception desk. "Hi," said Mariah. "I'm Mariah Miller, here for my first day!" She handed the woman the permission slips her mom had signed.

"Ah, " said the woman, "you must be the new intern."

Intern. It all sounded so important.

"Dr. Waters told me to send you down to the tanks when you got here." She gave Mariah directions and sent her on her way.

Mariah skipped down the long driveway feeling like Dorothy in the *Wizard of Oz*, only instead of this being the Yellow Brick Road, she thought, it was the Golden Opportunity Driveway. There were buildings to her left and buildings to her right, all old houses that had been taken over by the Lab. She had gone exploring down there a few times, but she had felt like a trespasser. Now she belonged there. Her directions were to go all the way down the driveway to the last building.

Bright sun filtered through the tall trees, and she stopped for a moment to look up into the canopy of lacy branches. A couple of crows called to each other as they sailed across. She smiled to think of what Crow had said about the happiness of giving. And now, she was going to give every Monday, Tuesday and Thursday of her summer vacation to the Lab. And, since time is an illusion, she thought, then what was it that she was giving?

When she opened the heavy door of the tank building she was met with a bouquet of salty, fishy, moldy smells. The subdued light and bubbling, whooshing sounds made her feel as though she were under water. A fogged up skylight cast a greenish haze that was reflected all over the walls and ceiling by the pools of moving water. She peered into a tank. It looked empty. "Hello," she called, wondering if she was in the right place.

Something splashed in the big tank across the room. A seal's dog-like face popped up, surprising her. It looked just like that harbor seal, Sivart, who had teased her and tricked her into saying Travis was her brother.

"Oh, hello, " she said.

The seal winked at her.

"Do I know you?" she said suspiciously. Of course, this seal could not talk to her. Since she had given away the spearhead, no animals had answered her quiet voice.

Just then the door on the bay side opened, shooting a path of bright light across the cement floor. A small man with a bucket and hip boots bustled in, oblivious to Mariah's presence. He looked like a leprechaun with freckled face, round cheeks, and pointy ears. His wild hair that had once been red but was now a yellowish white, toppled over horn-rimmed eyeglasses that looked as foggy as the old skylight. He mumbled something to himself, and went over to a clipboard and started writing on it.

"Hi," said Mariah, but the man did not seem to hear her and just went on writing.

Suddenly, the seal popped up and yipped. "Just a minute," said the man.

Mariah went to the edge of the tank and waited. She didn't want to interrupt. The seal seemed to be waiting, too. They both watched the faded green back of the man's tee shirt like is was a TV and they were waiting for the show to come on.

The seal made a small whine like a dog begging for a treat.

"Be patient," said the man, "I'll be right with you." And when he turned around, instead of just seeing a seal, he saw Mariah. He cleared his throat and looked embarrassed that she had witnessed him unaware.

"Oh, hello," he said, "May I help you?"

"No," said Mariah, "I'm the one who is supposed to ask you that." She went forward and reached out to shake his hand just as her parents had taught her. The man looked at his crusty hand, dusted it off on his pants, and offered it to her. "I'm Mariah Miller, the intern." She just loved the sound of that word.

He introduced himself as Dr. Waters, "You can call me Dr. Sam, or just Sam." The seal whined and made begging noises behind them. "Well, Mariah Miller, welcome. You're just in time," he said as he reached for the bucket. "Just in time to feed this rascal."

"Why is he here? He doesn't look sick."

"We got him just last week. He was at death's door."

The seal tipped his head and put his eyelids at half-mast for effect.

"What a ham," said Dr. Sam. "I could swear he understands what we're saying."

The seal and Mariah shared a sly grin. "Is he wounded? I don't see any marks."

"He had eaten a plastic bag, and we had to relieve him of the obstruction," said Dr. Waters, making a grimace as if he smelled a foul odor. "Thousands of seals, and tens of thousands of other animals like turtles and dolphins and whales are killed every year by those damn plastic shopping bags. Pardon my language."

Mariah remembered how she had saved that sea creature all tangled up in litter in the streamtime. She smiled and shrugged, "No problem," she said.

"Most seals are pretty picky about what they swallow, but not this one."

Mariah looked over at the seal who seemed to shrug his shoulders as if to say, "What can I say? It looked like food to me."

"He's still a bit dehydrated."

"Dehydrated? How can something that lives in water get dehydrated?"

"Water, water everywhere, but not a drop to drink," said Dr. Sam. "A seal gets his water from the food he eats, and surprisingly, saltwater fish are not very salty at all.

"How is that?" asked Mariah.

"Their osmoregulatory system."

"Osmo – what?"

"Think osmosis. It's the system that balances salts and eliminates waste from the bloodstream."

"Osmo-regulatory," repeated Mariah.

"Gills, guts and kidneys," said Dr. Sam.

Kidneys had never been so important as they had become in the past few months, and now, fish kidneys! "My dad just had a kidney transplant," Mariah said.

"How's he doing?

The seal bobbed up and down frantically trying to get their attention.

"Fine. He hasn't rejected it, and he'll be home soon. He'll have to be on a special diet."

"Well, this guy was on a special diet, but not a good one. That plastic bag made him very sick and unable to eat. Usually, if food is scarce seals make water from their fat, but if they're really sick they get dehydrated.

"He'll be taking a trip up to the Aquarium with Dr. Stein, spend a few weeks up there showing off before he's released. You can come along. He'll be the poster boy for the anti-plastic bag movement. He's quite a showoff."

The seal kept popping up and yearning for the contents of the bucket. "What kind of fish are those," she asked. "They like smelt, don't they?"

"My, my, Miss Mariah, he said, "Have you been studying for this job?"

"Kind of," she said, and winked at the seal who winked back at her and whimpered again.

"These are herring, one of his favorites.

"Okay, fella," he said, grabbing a slippery fish from the bucket and tossing it into the tank. The seal lunged at it making a splash, but had to dive down to get it. In just seconds he was back up and begging for more.

"This seal looks just like the one I met out on the marsh in March," she said.

"It's likely the same one. This guy was hanging around all winter, sunning himself on the dock like he was at a tropical resort." Dr. Waters held the bucket out to Mariah. She reached in and grabbed a fish. Even though it felt cold and yucky in her hand, she didn't make a face. This was her job, she thought, so she had to be very professional about it. The fish flopped back and forth and nearly slipped from her grasp. "Here you go," she said as she tossed the herring high up into the air over the tank. The seal leapt straight for it and caught it before it hit the water.

Dr. Sam clapped his hands. "You two are quite a team! They're going to love this act at the Aquarium! Marvelous Mariah and...hmm..." He scratched his chin. "We haven't given him a name yet. Would you like to do the honors?"

"Oh yes," said Mariah, remembering Sivart spelling his name, T, R, A... "I'd like to name him Traviss, with two S's," she said, and then with little hesitation, she added, "after my brother."

"Okay," said Dr. Sam. "Terrific Travis with two S's it is."

What a day! I love being an intern. Sivart, Traviss the seal was there! Dr. Sam let me name him. He didn't know I already knew his name. That's a secret. I added the second S for Seal, so he won't be confused with Travis the human. And I got to feed him. In fact, one of my jobs is feeding him on the days I go to the lab. I clean the tanks, too. Traviss ate a plastic bag and got real sick and dehydrated. People should be more careful with their trash.

Today I learned that if fish didn't have kidneys then seals couldn't eat them because they'd be too salty and the seals would be dehydrated. I never could have imagined how important such a little thing like a fish kidney could be. In fact, every little thing is important. Everything depends on everything else. Everything really is related. I think that's what the animals were talking about. Now I understand what they meant.

We're not just brothers and sisters in this

watery world, we are all part of each other, and we all need each other just like a seal needs a fish that's not too salty, and peeps need horseshoe crab eggs to eat, and the people in the ice age needed the horseshoe crab to stay alive when they were starving, and how they needed telsons for spears to catch fish.

Dr. Sam said I can go with them when they take Traviss to the Aquarium in Boston. We went out for water samples. I cleaned the tanks and got all wet and slimy. We tested the water and it was okay. We made fish popsicles for Traviss to eat. Since they float he has fun with them. Dr. Sam is teaching me how to put data in the computer. Next Tuesday we are going to Woods Hole on Cape Cod. Dr. Sam is taking me down there in a van with some other kids. They do joint projects. I can't wait!

Chapter XIV
True Blue

Mariah was so excited about her trip to Woods Hole she could hardly sleep. Earlier in the day she had found out that her dad was coming home any time now. She didn't want to be away when he arrived, but she really didn't want to miss the trip. When she spoke to him on the phone, he said, "You just go. I'll get home when I get home, and you can tell me all about it."

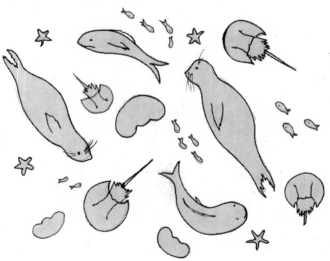

Her dreams were restless, as her mind went in and out of old nows and imagined ones. As she tossed and turned, kidneys and fishes and seals and horseshoe crabs drifted around and around on the floor of her consciousness.

Armed with her lunch bag, smeared with sunscreen, and ready to go, Mariah kissed her mom and headed out the door. She skipped up the street to the lab, and seeing the red van parked in the driveway with its doors open, she broke into a run.

"Hey, what's your hurry?" said Dr. Sam.

"I didn't want to be late."

He looked at his watch. "You're nearly a half-hour early," he said. "Run down to the tanks and check on your friend. Throw him a fish popsicle from the freezer, would you?"

"Sure," said Mariah. In just a few days she had come to feel at home in the tank building. It was part of her neighborhood now. When the tide wasn't too high she could walk down her lane, hop on the beach, and be at the tank house in seconds.

She opened the door to the magical, bubbling world. Traviss popped up to greet her.

"Hello, my friend," she said remembering the first time she had met him out on the cold marsh. As her hand went for the freezer's handle, Traviss bobbed up and down in anticipation.

"Hey, you're a seal, not a porpoise," she teased.

She reached into the freezer, got one of the fish

popsicles she had made the day before, and plopped it into the tank It floated like a big ice cube. Traviss dove down, came up under it, and ferried it around the tank as if it were a toy boat in a bathtub. He would have to play with it for a while until it was thawed out enough to eat. "Have fun," she said as she headed out the door and back up the hill.

When she got to the van, a couple of teenagers were joking around waiting to leave. Dr. Sam introduced them as James and Tom, and said they were thinking of studying marine biology when they went to college.

"Me, too," said Mariah.

She sat up front with Dr. Sam as they drove down the highway and over the Sagamore Bridge. Mariah remembered the words *Sagamore* and *Sachem,* and somehow knew they meant king or chief, but she couldn't remember just how she knew it.

"Are we there yet?" said the boys, like a couple of impatient kids in the back seat.

"We'll be there soon enough," said Dr. Sam.

As they approached Woods Hole on a twisting road, Dr. Sam pointed out campus buildings. When they reached the waterfront, Mariah could not believe how big it all seemed. They drove down the narrow street, large buildings on their right, and the water on their left, with important-looking research ships tied to the wharf. A ship jutted out into the blue water with the big letters NOAA painted on its prow. "NOAA, what's that, Dr. Sam?" asked Mariah.

"NOAA is the National Oceanic and Atmospheric

Administration. They keep us informed about the weather and what's happening with our planet."

Dr. Sam parked the van, and they went up a cobbled path and into a building to meet their guide. They took a tour of a research boat, visited a couple of labs where all sorts of things were happening: studies of seafloor samples, coastal pollution studies, and marine animal research. Mariah was confused by the vastness of all the science and overwhelmed with too much information when they finally ended up at the aquarium.

There were a couple of harbor seals in a tank out front. These seals didn't look very happy as they went round and round, in and out of sight in the aqua pool. The sign explained that they had been stranded and will never be released because they were unable to survive in the wild. Mariah leaned her face against the fencing mesmerized by their slow, rhythmic circling, when one of the seals slid up onto a platform. He wasn't as fat as Traviss, and his coat wasn't as velvety. He met Mariah's eyes. "Hello, brother," she whispered.

The seal slipped back into the water and disappeared. The boys stood by the open door and called for her to go inside.

As they walked though the aquarium looking at all the different kinds of fish and sea life, Dr. Sam rushed them along saying they had one more stop to make before they headed back home.

They tromped up the stairs to another part of the

aquarium, the part where the backsides of the tanks were, the part that the public didn't see in regular aquariums. But this aquarium was different. People were supposed to see the insides of it. There was a tidal pool petting tank for little kids. A couple of horseshoe crabs sat like stones among the hermit crabs and snails.

Dr. Sam didn't give them enough time to read all of the plaques. "Next stop, Associates of Cape Cod," he said as they headed for the van. "Mariah, you're going to find this particularly interesting."

Mariah didn't know what to expect when they pulled up in front of a shiny new office building. The boys in the back seat were confused, too. "Associates of Cape Cod," James read the sign. "What is this place?"

"You'll see," said Dr. Sam as they tumbled out of the van. Mariah saw a neat looking graphic of a horseshoe crab as they entered the sunny lobby.

"Dr. Waters, we've been expecting you," the receptionist said, picking up the phone. "Dr. Phillips, Dr. Waters is here, and he's brought three visitors with him." She pointed to a clipboard, motioning for them to sign in. "He'll be right down."

Mariah did a double take when Dr. Phillips came into the reception area to meet them. His skin was dark, his hair was black, and his high cheekbones and straight nose looked curiously familiar. Where had she seen him before? Although he was dressed in a crisp blue shirt and striped tie, he looked just like one of the Wampanoag men she had seen when she had gone to the first Thanksgiving. He looked just like Great Blue's father!

"Welcome to Associates of Cape Cod," he said.

"Mariah here is very interested in horseshoe crabs," said Dr. Sam.

"Well, you've come to the right place. If it weren't for horseshoe crabs, we wouldn't be here," said Dr. Phillips.

"Back in the 1950s, a scientist named Fred Bang discovered something very important about the horseshoe crab's blood. As you may know, horseshoe crabs were around millions of years before the dinosaurs. They're ancient, and they have an ancient immune system like no other animal in the world."

Mariah remembered the ice age, the coppery taste of the horseshoe crab blood in her mouth, and how Nelson had said they had been around for ages and ice ages. Chills of excitement ran through her.

"Cells in their blood called amebocytes react in a special way when they encounter bacteria. The cells coagulate; they stick together and form a clump around the bad stuff to keep it from invading the rest of the animal."

Dr. Phillips led them down a corridor. Pictures and diagrams of horseshoe crabs, test tubes, products, and white-suited laboratory workers lined the walls.

"Later, in the '70s, a microbiologist at Woods Hole named Stan Watson was using the solution made from the horseshoe crab's blood—limulus lysate—in his research on marine bacteria when he realized its potential value to the medical community. So, he started Associates of Cape Cod.

"Before the Limulus Amebocyte Lysate – LAL – test was developed, the only way to test for endotoxin, an indication of bacteria, was to use rabbits. Manufacturers of pharmaceuticals and medical devices would have to have thousands of bunnies available to inject with solutions to test for bacteria to make sure products were safe. If bacteria was present, the rabbits got a fever. As you can imagine, it took hours, even days, for the rabbits to get sick. The LAL test takes only minutes; it's simpler, cleaner, and drug makers and medical device manufacturers don't need to keep a herd of rabbits on hand for testing."

Mariah looked up at Dr. Phillips. "My dad had kidney dialysis and then a kidney transplant. Do they use the LAL test for that stuff?"

"Oh yes," he exclaimed. "All of the fluids that are used for dialysis get tested, and any intravenous equipment is tested, too. The artificial kidney device and tubing used to clean your dad's blood had to pass the LAL test. In fact, anyone who has had a vaccination or shot, an IV, or any organ or artificial device transplant can thank the horseshoe crab!"

Mariah's jaw dropped. She couldn't wait to tell her dad. He would never again say that horseshoe crabs were a nuisance.

James said, "So, when I had to get that hepatitis shot for school, it got tested?"

"It certainly did," said Dr. Phillips as he led them

through a metal door into a room with stainless steel racks stacked with lab suits. He handed them each a white jacket, a hairnet, and a facemask. "Here, put these on. The more sterile we are, the less likely we are to contaminate the product."

"This is cool," said Tom, "I feel like a doctor."

When they were all suited up Dr. Phillips led them through another door. Mariah could not believe what she saw. It looked like an operating room but instead of operating tables there were rows of shelves—not bookshelves—horseshoe crab shelves. The crabs were upside down with their telsons sticking up against a clear plastic barrier. They were all large horseshoe crabs, bigger than Nelson, and he was quite big. Lab workers scurried around.

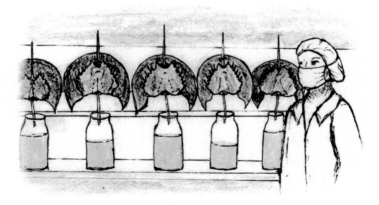

Beneath each crab was a bottle filled with a frothy blue liquid. "Oh my god, what are they doing to them?"

"Bleeding them so we can make the lysate," said Dr. Phillips.

"Does it hurt them?"

"I hope not."

"Does it kill them?"

"Horseshoe crabs are very valuable to us, so we do everything possible to keep them alive."

"How much blood do you take?"

"It's like people donating blood. We only take a percentage of their blood. And we don't bleed crabs if they've been injured or stressed from being collected or transported. We want to keep them healthy. We depend on them for our livelihood."

Mariah had heard that before. Remembering how the Peeps depend on their eggs, she said, "Migrating shorebirds like sandpipers depend on them, too."

You're right about that," he agreed.

"These crabs look bigger than most of the ones I see in Duxbury."

"These are females. They have to be at least eight inches across to be bled, and the females are the bigger ones." Dr. Phillips took them over to the staging area.

"These crabs have all been rinsed, measured and sorted." About a dozen big horseshoe crabs scrabbled and scraped on the bottom of a plastic bin, a sight Mariah found very disturbing.

A lab worker reached into the bin, brought out a crab and took it over to an empty bay on one of the shelves. They watched as she placed the crab on the shelf and positioned it so that the hinge that held the two parts of the shell was exposed. "Now she disinfects it with an alcohol wipe, just like they do at the doctor's," said Dr. Phillips.

Mariah had to turn away when the technician stuck the needle into the crab.

"That's got to hurt," she said as the blue blood dripped down into the bottle. The bottle already had clear fluid in it, and Dr. Phillips explained that it was an anti-coagulant solution. They watched as the technician took a crab from the shelf and placed it in another bin. Then she took the bottle of milky blue fluid and passed it through a window.

Mariah walked along the row of shelves looking at each crab individually. "Thank you," she said to each one. Dr. Sam and the boys laughed, and started thanking the crabs too.

One of the horseshoe crabs had a broken telson. Mariah was wondering if she might be a philanthropic crab like Nelson when she realized that all of the horseshoe crabs there, whether they knew it or not, were truly philanthropic.

"After the blood is collected," said Dr. Phillips as he led them through another door, "then it is put through a centrifuge where it gets spun around really fast to separate the amebocytes, the cells, from the serum."

A technician put two of the bottles into a cylinder, and went to get more. "After it's separated, we discard the serum and then concentrate the cells."

Mariah was hardly listening as Dr. Phillips pointed

to bottles aging in a refrigerator. They looked through a big window at the bottling plant where the lysate solution was being put into little bottles with labels. "Then we put the bottles in boxes and ship them out to drug companies, hospitals, and medical device manufacturers. And we also have a lab here where companies send samples to be tested."

"Don't some of the horseshoe crabs die from this?"

Dr. Phillips looked at her thoughtfully. "Yes, I'm afraid to say, some do. But because we know just how important the horseshoe crab is to us, we are working to stabilize and restore populations, and reduce deaths related to collecting and bleeding.

"Horseshoe crabs are also a favorite bait for the eel and conch fisheries. Scientists have developed artificial bait bags to substitute for real horseshoe crabs."

Mariah's lips trembled as she held back her tears. She stepped away and looked around so no one would notice.

"It wasn't long ago that there were bounties on them," said Dr. Phillips. They were thought to be a threat to the shellfish industry. Kids around Woods Hole would bring the telsons down to town hall and get paid a penny a piece for them. Humans have been decimating the population for quite some time now. Now we must protect them."

Mariah felt sick remembering the picture of Uncle Joe and his friends. She wanted to tell Dr. Phillips about Nelson. She wanted to make everyone in the world understand what she knew.

Dr. Phillips smiled kindly at them. "We'd all do better to remember the words of my grandfather: 'We do not inherit the earth from our ancestors, we borrow it from our children.'"

Those were the exact words Great Blue had said when he threw the handful of fish back. "Oh my goodness," exclaimed Mariah, "The People of the First Light!"

"That's right," said Dr. Phillips. "Native people honor all gifts of the Earth. The horseshoe crab today reminds us that it's in everyone's best interest, eh?" He smiled at Mariah. "We still have a lot to learn from old Limulus here," he said as he led them back out to the lobby to see them off.

The ride home was quiet as Mariah and the boys reflected on all they had seen. When the van finally pulled into the driveway, and they all hopped out, Dr. Sam said, "Mariah, could you run down to the tanks and feed your seal before you go home?"

"Sure," she said, thrilled that Dr. Sam had said *her* seal. It was four o'clock, feeding time. She said goodbye to the boys, thanked Dr. Sam for taking her on the trip, and headed down to the tank building.

When she opened the door a shaft of afternoon sunshine streamed across the floor and cast fresh light on the moving water in the tanks. A kaleidoscope of broken reflections, shards of green light, swirled around her.

Traviss popped up. He seemed thrilled to see her. Or was he just hungry?

She tossed him one fish at a time, then a squid, and he caught each one before it hit the water. Dr. Sam had said she could show the folks at the Aquarium in Boston what a talented catcher Traviss was when they took him up there next week.

Normally she liked to hang around the tank watching Traviss, *her seal,* doing seal things. But this afternoon was different. She wanted to get right home and share what she had learned at Associates of Cape Cod, so she marked the feeding sheet, went through the back door, and headed home along the beach.

Halfway between the Lab and her beach, she stopped dead in her tracks. There in the eelgrass, washed up in a row of seaweed, upside down, lay an old, dark brown horseshoe crab—with a broken telson.

She knelt down for a closer look, and reached out to turn it over. The limp legs hung heavy; their dead, waterlogged weight pulling the remains away from the shell. On the back part of its shell near the base of its telson, round craters marked where the barnacles once had lived. The piece of seaweed was gone, too. But there was no doubt in Mariah's mind.

She looked around to see a few other old horseshoe crab shells strewn along the tide line, realizing that each one had been as important as the next, each one as significant as the one she held in her hand.

Tears rolled down her cheeks. She shook Nelson's shell until the heavy legs and decomposing book gills fell to the sand.

Moving a few rocks aside, she used a clam shell to dig a hole, a hole shaped just like Nelson. Carefully, she placed the legs and gills into the hole, just as she had seen them when she first met Nelson alive and upside down.

Smiling and crying at the same time, she covered the remains, patted the sand down and made a little pyramid of stones. She took mussel shells and placed them like flower petals around the base.

Just then she heard a little peep, A sandpiper landed nearby, hopped a little closer, and, as if paying her respects, stood quietly by.

"Goodbye, Nelson," Mariah whispered through her tears. And deep in her heart she heard Nelson's kind voice say, *clear as the sky and true blue.*

She walked down to the water and rinsed out the hard brown shell. Letting her tears fall felt good. She wasn't crying so much from sadness, though she was sad. These tears were a new kind of tears. They were tears of completeness, of change and transition; tears of love and acceptance.

She remembered what Aaron's son, Lloyd, had said, and as she shook the water from the shell, she was grateful, for if she had never found the spearhead, and never talked to Nelson, she never would have learned what she had learned on that day.

All that remained of Nelson may have seemed like

an old brown shell, but Mariah knew he would always live in her heart.

Drying her tears with the sleeve of her shirt, Mariah hung Nelson's smelly old shell on a nail in the garage, and then ran through the mudroom into the house.

"Anybody home?" she called.

"I am!" said her dad, who was lounging on the couch in the living room. He reached out so she could give him a big hug and kiss. "My, you smell fishy."

"Marine biology is a fishy business," she said.

She told him the whole story of her trip to Woods Hole, barely taking a breath she was so excited, and saving the part about Associates of Cape Cod for last. She ran out to the garage and got Nelson's carapace.

"Phew, that stinks," said her dad.

She bent the two pieces of the shell, pointing to the center of the hinge, "the cardiac membrane," she said, showing him just how they were bled, and explaining about the amebocytes and LAL test.

"So," she said, "You have horseshoe crabs to thank for your life!"

Her dad assured her, "I will never, ever again make a disparaging remark about a horseshoe crab. I promise!"

I dedicate this journal to my friend Nelson Telson the horseshoe crab. He was a great animal. I will miss him. R.I.P. Nelson. You are true blue!

Today was one of the most important days of my life. We went to Woods Hole and then to the Associates of Cape Cod. And Dad came home from the hospital. I found out that if it wasn't for horseshoe crabs, Dad might not still be alive, since all of the kidney dialysis stuff had to be tested by this LAL test made from horseshoe crab blood.

I remember Nelson saying that horseshoe crabs were Fifth Business on the planet. He said they were always around in the background, never starring in a leading role, but some stories couldn't begin or end without them. I never really understood what that meant, so tonight I kicked Travis off the computer and looked up Fifth Business.

It said this: "Those roles which, being neither those of Hero or Heroine, Confidante nor Villain, but which were nonetheless essential to bring about the Recognition or the dénouement, were called the Fifth Business in drama and opera companies organized according to the old style; the player who acted these parts was often referred to as Fifth Business." I had to look up *dénouement* too. It means the resolution or ending of a story.

Well, Nelson and all of the other horseshoe crabs aren't fifth business at all. Not only did they save Daddy's life but the lives of thousands of bunnies! Today I learned that they are heroes. Scientists are discovering new things about them every day. Dr. Phillips told us that scientists study their eyes because they are so ancient. And they might even be able to make an AIDS vaccine from part of the blood. There's this stuff called chitin they get from the shells, and it's used to make special thread for stitches and bandages that dissolve like the ones they used for Dad's operation. They even put it in toothpaste!

Another thing I found out is that there aren't nearly as many horseshoe crabs around as there should be since people have been killing them just to kill them like Uncle Joe and his friends did.

They also kill a lot of them for fertilizer and eel bait and they'd better cut it out.

Also I learned that the People of the First Light used them for fertilizer, and they showed the Plymouth colonists, and that helped them grow the crops and survive in the beginning.

Dr. Phillips said that humans need to stop killing the horseshoe crabs or there won't be enough to make the lysate – that's the stuff they use to test all the medical gadgets and medicines *to make sure they're safe.*

All this got me to thinking. If something like the horseshoe crab could seem so unimportant for so long, I bet there are millions of other things in the world that people might be killing without knowing that they could be killing themselves by doing it!

Dr. Sam said I'm an environmentalist, but I know what I really am. Like Nelson and Aaron and Lloyd and Traviss, I'm just another creature in this watery world.

THE END

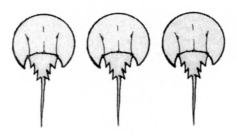

ACKNOWLEDGEMENTS

The writing of this book took place over a period of nine years. Then it rested in the mud for a while. I referred to many books, articles, and web sites for information about horseshoe crabs, medicine, relativity theory, the first Thanksgiving, and the Wampanoag People.

Articles especially helpful were *The Changeless Horseshoe Crab* by Anne and Jack Rudloe, National Geographic, April 1981; *Facing Extinction After 350 Million Years?* by Greg O'Brien, Cape Cod View, 20 July, 2000; *Of Crabs and Men* by Dyke Hendrickson, Mass High Tech 2/9/2004; The *Horseshoe Crab* by Patty Sturtevant, Ph.D. of Sarasota Marine Lab. Patty was also kind enough to correspond via email and answer any questions I had. The re-peeps joke was hers.

A Rip in Time by Stephen Reucroft and John Swain, Boston Globe, January 3, 2000 helped with the time travel and relativity theory. Plimoth Plantation's October, 2000 magazine provided *A New Look at an Old Myth* about the first harvest and thanksgiving traditions.

Books included *Crab Wars* by William Sargent, University Press of New England 2002; *The Crab that Crawled Out of the Past* by Lorus and Margery Milne, Antheneum, 1967; *Wood's Vocabulary of Massachusett* by William Wood, Evolution Publishing 2002. A special shout out to Roberston Davies' novel, *Fifth Business,* for the concept and definition Mariah finds on the Internet, which appears to be an historical fictional quote created by that author.

Among Web references too numerous to list, www.horseshoecrab.org was especially helpful.

Bob Hillman at Battelle Labs in Duxbury read the book in its early stages and pointed me to Dr. Michael Dawson at the Associates of Cape Cod who answered my questions about blood collection and manufacture, and uses of LAL.

Great teachers deserve recognition. No matter how old I get, I'll always cherish the validation I got from Tony Chamberlain and Inga Karetnikova.

Very special thanks to Clare Applegate, Jane Bennett, Carolyn Eringhaus, Paula Marcoux, Jamie Stevens, Anna Colavito, Selden Tearse, Monique Attinger, Brian Lies, Nancy Richard, Mary Farrell, Leslie Lewis-Helgeson, and my best friend in the whole wide world, Patsy Hamel for sharing your sharp eyes, fine sensibilities, and unique points of view while giving me much-needed encouragement along the way. And biggest thanks to Jim, my twenty-four/seven partner in creative endeavors, who is always there with wild ideas, astute criticism and discerning taste. His favorite word is "inexorable" and since it didn't make it into the book I'll use it here: Although it took years to bring Nelson Telson to the world's attention, his eventual renown was inexorable.